LAST STOP

OTHER LIVING DEAD PRESS BOOKS

THE TURNING: A STORY OF THE LIVING DEAD * MEN OF PERDITION
THE DEAD OF SPACE BOOK 1 AND 2 * THE BABYLONIAN CURSE
PLAYING GOD: A ZOMBIE NOVEL * THE JUNKYARD
THE UNNATURAL DEAD * SHADOWS OF MEN
SUPERHEROES VS. ZOMBIES
MY LITTLE SISTER'S A ZOMBIE
ETERNAL AFTERMATH: A ZOMBIE NOVEL
PLANET OF THE DEAD 1&2 * THE HAUNTED THEATRE
ZOMBIES IN OUR HOMETOWN
UNITED STATES OF ARMAGEDDON
THE Z WORD * REVIEWS OF THE DEAD
NIGHT OF THE WOLF: A WEREWOLF ANTHOLOGY
JUST BEFORE NIGHT: A ZOMBIE ANTHOLOGY
THE BOOK OF HORROR 1 & 2
THE WAR AGAINST THEM: A ZOMBIE NOVEL
CHILDREN OF THE VOID * DARK DREAMS
BLOOD RAGE & DEAD RAGE (BOOK 1& 2 OF THE RAGE VIRUS SERIES)
DEAD MOURNING: A ZOMBIE HORROR STORY
BOOK OF THE DEAD: A ZOMBIE ANTHOLOGY VOLUME 1-6
LOVE IS DEAD: A ZOMBIE ANTHOLOGY
ETERNAL NIGHT: A VAMPIRE ANTHOLOGY
END OF DAYS: AN APOCALYPTIC ANTHOLOGY VOLUME 1-5
DEAD HOUSE: A ZOMBIE GHOST STORY
THE ZOMBIE IN THE BASEMENT (FOR ALL AGES)
THE LAZARUS CULTURE: A ZOMBIE NOVEL
DEAD WORLDS: UNDEAD STORIES VOLUMES 1-7
FAMILY OF THE DEAD * REVOLUTION OF THE DEAD
KINGDOM OF THE DEAD * DEAD HISTORY
THE MONSTER UNDER THE BED * DEAD THINGS
DEAD TALES: SHORT STORIES TO DIE FOR
ROAD KILL: A ZOMBIE TALE * DEADFREEZE * DEADFALL
SOUL EATER * THE DARK * RISE OF THE DEAD
ZOMBIES AND POWER TOOLS
DEAD END: A ZOMBIE NOVEL * VISIONS OF THE DEAD
THE CHRONICLES OF JACK PRIMUS
INSIDE THE PERIMETER: SCAVENGERS OF THE DEAD
BOOK OF CANNIBALS VOLUME 2 * CHRISTMAS IS DEAD…AGAIN
EMAILS OF THE DEAD * CHILDREN OF THE DEAD
TALES OF THE DEAD * TALES OF BIGFOOT
THE END: A ZOMBIE NOVEL * NOVELLAS OF THE DEAD

THE DEADWATER SERIES
DEADWATER * DEADWATER: Expanded Edition
DEADRAIN * DEADCITY * DEADWAVE * DEAD HARVEST
DEAD UNION * DEAD VALLEY * DEAD TOWN/ HOMEWARD BOUND
DEAD GRAVE * DEAD SALVATION * DEAD ARMY (Deadwater series book 10)

LAST STOP

ANTHONY GIANGREGORIO

LAST STOP

ISBN Softcover   ISBN 13: 978-1-61199-043-0
                  ISBN 10: 1-611990-432

This is a work of fiction.
Names, characters, places and incidents either are the product of the author's imagination or are used fictitiously, and any resemblance to any actual persons, living or dead, events, or locales is entirely coincidental.

This book was printed in the United States of America.

For more info on obtaining additional copies of this book, contact:
www.livingdeadpress.com

Last Stop originally published in Dark Places by Living Dead Press

Visit the author on Facebook

LAST STOP

The Boston subway system is one of the oldest underground train systems in the world. In the past two hundred years, the tunnels have slowly grown into hundreds of miles of twisting, turning shafts of darkness; cut into the earth like jagged cylinders, like crystals constantly growing until they threaten to consume their entire surroundings.

Tunnels have been closed and others added. Sometimes in the interest of progress, new tunnels are built under old ones, the subway system constantly burrowing deeper and deeper into the earth like a bunch of manic moles.

Sometimes, man goes too far.

Sometimes things better left undisturbed can be awakened.

And once awakened, it's possible these things may never rest again.

* * *

Jonathan Ramsey sighed and shifted the weight of his young son onto his other hip. His son was going on five and was starting to get heavy. Either that or Jonathan was getting older and just couldn't manage to carry his growing son like he had when he was first born.

Walking into Government Center, he slid his T pass into the slot and pushed through the turnstile.

He glanced into the ticket booth where there would normally be a ticket agent for the subway, but true to form, it was empty. He checked his watch one more time to make sure he wouldn't be late for the last train out of Boston for the night.

It was 12:45 a.m.

Good, he still had fifteen minutes.

Walking down the wide stairwell with a metal railing in the middle, he headed down to the platform that would take him home; to his house and empty bed.

But first he would have to reach his waiting car, parked at Wellington Station in Medford, and then drive home another twenty minutes that would see him pulling into his driveway.

This was supposed to have been his day off, and so he had given the babysitter some much needed time off as well. He had been called in to work to fix some problem with the server.

Though he hadn't wanted to, he really had no choice in the matter, and so had brought his son with him, letting the boy play with a few action figures he kept in his desk drawer for just such an occurrence.

He was a widower, his wife dying in a fatal car accident over a year ago.

Now it was just him and his son, Billy. He looked down at the angelic face of his sleeping son, the boy's head resting on his shoulder, while he walked onto the train platform and sighed.

Even at his son's young age, Jonathan could see so much of his wife in the boy's face.

Billy was all he had left of the love of his life. Billy had been the only thing keeping him grounded when he had found out that fateful night a year ago that his wife was dead.

He had been so overcome with loss, he had reached the point he may have actually eaten his gun, the one he kept in a lockbox under his bed, but then Billy had come into the bedroom and asked what was wrong.

Realizing he had to stay strong for his son, he had placed the revolver back into his bureau draw and had never looked back.

He had a son, dammit!

He couldn't afford to be so selfish, to kill himself, even if it would end his pain.

Then what would happen to Billy?

He had hugged his son and had delicately tried to explain the nuances of his mother never coming back. That Billy would never see her alive again, but would see her in Heaven some day, that she was waiting for them both.

Billy had, of course, cried, and the two of them had sat on her side of the bed and cried together long into the night until both of them had finally succumbed to exhaustion and had fallen into a restless slumber.

Now, almost a year later, he had learned to manage his grief, only now the loss would sneak up on him at odd times, usually in the middle of the night when he would get up to use the bathroom.

He would return from the bathroom and sometimes see her hump of a sleeping body on her side of the bed, but then he would blink and the mirage would disappear like a light snow falling on warm asphalt.

The sound of the train approaching pulled him from his reverie and he took a step toward the painted red line that lined the edge of the platform. It was two feet away from the edge, actually, and he had learned long ago not to cross it.

A regular denizen of the city, he had heard countless horror stories about men and women getting struck by the train or just plain falling off the platform, sometimes pushed, to be ground into putty by the train's metal wheels.

And then there were all those stories about the third rail.

Checking around to make sure no one was near him, he waited as the train slowed and came to a halt. The platform was far from empty and he studied the few other people waiting for the train with him.

There was a young woman, around his age waiting near the tunnel that would lead to the other side of the station. She had brown hair and a pretty face.

She was covered by a heavy jacket and so he couldn't see if she was trim or fat, not that it mattered really, but he was still a male and would admire beauty when he came across it.

On his opposite side was a man in his late forties. He wore a three-piece suit and a gray overcoat over his outfit. In his right hand was a briefcase and in his left was a cell phone, which the man was actively using, his voice echoing off the dirty tile walls.

The man had his hand to his ear, and Jonathan couldn't help but admire the handsome timepiece he wore on his wrist.

That was how you got mugged on the subway, flashing that kind of bling around. Jonathan couldn't help but wonder who the man could be talking to so late at night.

Perhaps a girlfriend or wife maybe?

The train came to a stop on the platform, the wind of its arrival ruffling Billy's hair. Jonathan brushed the few errant blonde hairs that fell over his son's eyes and prepared to enter the car.

The doors opened with a lilting, *cling, clang*, and then he was inside.

The operator of the train, a few cars up in his stall, mumbled the next stop into the speaker and then the train was off once more.

Jonathan sat near one of the doors, gazing out the tinted, tempered glass windows. As the train rocked back and forth gently, like a sea-going vessel, he couldn't help but read the advertisements spread out overhead on the curved corners of where the ceiling met the walls.

He was a captive audience after all, just as the advertisers knew he would be. He saw an ad for Night College. Earn a degree in his spare time, it read in bold letters. Another one told all who read it of equality, no matter what the color of their skin or ethnic background; reminding him of Sesame Street for some strange reason.

Maybe it was because he watched the show so often with his son. He didn't mind it actually, remembering it from when he was a kid. But Barney was another story. That show made him want to shoot himself in the head all over again but for very different reasons.

Looking back up at the ads, he saw another one was for some cleaning solution that did everything but make you dinner.

He closed his eyes and stopped reading, though the pictures still seemed to spin around inside his head.

Deciding he wouldn't be resting anytime soon, he opened his eyes and decided to people-watch a little. Across from him, five seats up, was an older man in his late seventies.

He was wearing a plaid coat and his nose was buried in a newspaper. Despite the man's advanced age, he looked fit, the hands holding the newspaper strong, not looking frail and thin like many other men of his similar age.

He had a long face like a Bassett hound and his hair was brown with a few streaks of gray that only made him look more mature, or scholarly.

Jonathan looked to his right to gaze at the two remaining passengers in his particular car. The first was a young business woman in a gray power suit, her hair tied up in a bun. She sat with an open folder in her lap. If Jonathan was right, she looked like a lawyer or perhaps a legal aide. She had on a pair of slim wire glasses and despite the professional getup, she was beautiful.

The second passenger was very obviously a bum or homeless person. He was stretched out at the front of the car, his body covering five seats, and he was snoring contently, his back to anyone who was watching him.

The woman in the power suit crossed her legs, one of the pant legs riding up to show a large amount of well-toned skin. Jonathan stared at the shapely leg, admiring the contours. If her leg was that attractive, then what would the rest of her look like unclothed?

For just a moment, Jonathan felt something in his loins he hadn't felt in almost a year. Feeling dirty for even thinking such a thing, still too much in love with his late wife to even consider dating, he turned away to gaze back out the dark windows; nothing on the other sides of them but stone as the train shot through the miles of tunnels.

The train slowed at its next stop and the doors swung open with the expected *cling, clang*.

No one entered his car, but when he glanced through the windows at the rear of the car and into the next one, he saw two teenagers wearing black leather coats step aboard. One carried a guitar case and the other a paper bag with the writing, *Newbury Comics* on it.

He knew there was one near State Street and figured the boys must have shopped there earlier in the night.

As the train pulled away from the platform, the two boys laughed and sat down; talking together about God knew what. The train operator muffled the next stop into the speaker.

Jonathan looked away then, remembering what it was like to be seventeen with the world in front of him, all the potentials of life like fruit from a tree just waiting to be plucked.

He looked down at the face of his sleeping son and decided things weren't so bad. Sure, he had lost his wife, but at least he still had his son.

The door separating one car from another opened with a loud thump and a man in a Transit cop's uniform stepped through. He was tall, slightly over six feet, definitely, and his wide shoulders and muscular forearms—easily discernable under his leather jacket—only added to the picture of masculinity and confidence.

His heavy black work boots echoed in the empty car as he moved down the center aisle. As the man moved closer, Jonathan's eyes went like a magnet to the handgun holstered to his belt. The cop had a radio on his belt and frivolous chatter could be heard coming from it; though hard to make out clearly with the noise of the rolling train.

When the cop reached Jonathan, he nodded politely, actually smiling slightly at the sight of the sleeping boy in Jonathan's arms.

Now that he was closer, Jonathan looked again at the man's handgun and the picture of a steer that was embossed on the holster.

Then the cop was at the next door for the following car. He stopped and glared down at the bum, but did nothing, leaving the sleeping man alone. Then he opened the door and slid through.

Jonathan watched him talk to the two teenagers in the next car for a few seconds and then move on. One of the boys gave the cop the finger when the large man's back was to him and despite himself, Jonathan found himself chuckling at the sight.

The older man across from him looked up from his newspaper, wondering what was so amusing, but when Jonathan smiled at him and controlled himself, quieting his snickering, the man went back to his paper, digging his nose into the folds of pulp like a dog seeking warmth in the creases of a blanket.

With nothing much to hold his attention, Jonathan closed his eyes and tried to rest again. The gentle rocking of the train lulled him into a false sense of security, and only the weight of his son on top of him kept him from sleeping.

The train pulled into the next stop and the doors opened wide. Seconds ticked by, but no one boarded. Then, just as the doors began to close, Jonathan heard voices on the platform and looked up to see three more passengers step into the car behind him. The one with the two teenagers in it.

The doors closed and the train began rolling again. As the train left the station, Jonathan looked up at the map on the wall. They had just left the last stop in the city, Aquarium station now behind them.

The next stop would be six miles away, the tunnel actually going deep underground as it made its way to the suburbs.

Jonathan studied the three new passengers. Two were male and one was female, all different ages ranging from twenty to forty.

They were all Spanish, and if Jonathan had to guess, he would have figured they were a few of the thousands of workers that went into Boston every night as part of the hundreds of cleaning crews that would clean the buildings after the office workers had gone home for the night.

In his building alone, there were more than twenty cleaners, all happy people who seemed to work hard and enjoyed their jobs.

He smiled as he watched them in the next car.

They were all talking together, but due to the divider of the car doors, all he could see was their mouths moving and sometimes their hands waving as they tried to make a point with one another.

The teenage boys were quiet now, as they too, watched the three newcomers in their car.

Jonathan leaned back and tried to relax. It would be fifteen or twenty minutes before the train reached Wellington station.

He closed his eyes and tried to get comfortable when he began to feel a rumbling.

At first he just assumed it was the car rolling along, but he soon realized it was something else. As he looked around the car, he saw the pretty woman in the power suit and the old man also looking around, trying to discern the cause of the rumbling.

As for the bum, he still slept, blissfully unaware of his surroundings.

Jonathan was sitting upright in his seat now, but all there was to see was the blackness outside the glass windows.

They were now a mile or so from the station they had departed and at least a few hundred feet underground, the train still rolling along.

Then a mighty roar filled the inside of the car, sounding like an earthquake or a bomb had gone off, and the car seemed to jump off the tracks.

Jonathan reached out, grabbing a nearby pole—put there for just such an occurrence—when a loud screeching sound filled the car, tearing apart the white noise of the train's wheels rolling on the tracks.

The train lurched forward, throwing Jonathan and the other passengers across the car like feathers in the wind.

Something heavy fell on top of the car in front of the one he was in, and the entire world seemed to explode with light and sound.

Petrified, not understanding what was happening, he cradled Billy to his chest and rolled across the floor, his back coming up hard against the door at the front of the car. Glass shattered in some of the small, five inch upper windows as the car twisted on its frame.

Yelling filled his ears and he wondered if it was his voice or one of the other passengers in the car with him. Billy woke up then, screaming in fright as he saw there was something terribly wrong with his world.

Another body struck him, slamming into him hard and Jonathan wondered which of his other passengers it could have been.

The lights in the car had flicked off and there was only darkness.

At first he thought there was nothing but silence surrounding him, but then he realized it wasn't that there was no noise, it was just that the amount of noise had decreased exponentially.

There was still a slight rumbling coming from both sides of the car he was in.

Not knowing what could possibly be happening, he lay still, holding his son, squeezing the small body tightly, trying to soothe him.

His shoulder ached from where he struck the door and he gritted his teeth, sucking up the pain. He needed to be strong for his son; at least until he knew what was happening.

The only thing he could think of that could have happened, was that the train had somehow become derailed, the entire train, cars and all, actually jumping the tracks to fall onto the rocks and stone of the tunnel floor.

There were moans of pain surrounding him, but with no lights, he could see nothing. But then small lights on the ceiling, and a few scattered near the floor, flickered on. Small emergency lights filled the car with a diffuse yellow glow. Dust clouds filled the car, smoke swirling in the circumference of the emergency lights' glow, and he had his first look at who had slid into him.

It was the old man.

The man had a small bruise on his forehead, but other than that appeared to be unharmed. With his free right hand, Jonathan gently pushed the man off him and to the side, letting the man's head slump onto his shoulder.

With the lights on, though dim, he was able to see that the car was still upright, though at a slight angle. Billy was still crying in his arms and he patted his head, telling him everything would be fine. Though he said this, he honestly prayed it would be so.

Another loud crashing sound came from somewhere outside the car and he felt the train rumble and vibrate from the shock.

Vivid images of thousands of tons of earth falling through the roof to bury the train and all who were in it flooded into his mind, but he tried to keep those frightening images at bay. Billy stirred in his arms again, burying his head deeper into his chest.

Not knowing what else to do, he hugged his son tighter, wishing by his will alone he could make sure Billy stayed safe.

Next to him, the old man was stirring, groaning, as he came back to the world of consciousness.

"Oh my God, what the hell happened?" he asked in a daze as he looked around the cockeyed train car.

"Don't know," Jonathan said. "I was just thinking the same thing myself."

From across the car, lying on the seats, was the woman in the power suit. She sat up, brushing her hair from her forehead as she tried to fix her suit, as if at a time like this how she looked mattered.

"It doesn't matter what happened," she stated briskly. "All we need to do is wait here for help to arrive. And let me tell you, someone's in for a lawsuit."

The old man chuckled at the first part of the woman's comment.

"Oh, you think so, do you? Listen to me, young lady, it's one o' clock in the morning. It's gonna take time for them to get to us. And while we're waiting, the whole damn tunnel could fall down on top of us. Thanks, but I think I'll see to myself. If I can make it through WW2, I think I can get out of here in one piece."

The woman pursed her lips in distaste, the inflection aimed at the old man. "You can do whatever the hell you want, mister, but I'm staying here."

Jonathan decided to try and keep the peace. "Look, please, both of you. Why don't we at least see what's happening before we go off half-cocked," he pleaded.

The old man frowned at him, but otherwise stayed quiet, deciding to inventory his body for damage.

As for the woman, she went back to fussing with her suit; brushing dust off her clothing like it would turn into acid and eat through to her skin if she didn't remove it quickly.

Jonathan tried to see through the glass windows of the car, hoping to see what had happened to them, but the black tint made it all but impossible.

Every few seconds, a few sparks could be seen as a torn wire flashed and flickered in the darkness of the tunnel.

Billy was stirring in his arms and he looked down at his son's small face.

"Hey, how you doin'? Better I hope?" he asked his son.

Sniffling with bouts of hitched breaths, Billy nodded yes.

"I'm okay, Daddy. What happened? Did we crash? I thought there wasn't stuff down here that could hit us like when we drive in the car. You said so."

Jonathan smiled down at his son, wiping a tear off Billy's cheek with his sleeve.

"Yeah, son, I know I did. We just need to wait for help to arrive and then we'll be fine, you'll see."

"Yeah, right, you hope so. What if everyone has gone home or snuck out early and no one knows we're down here?" the old man asked accusingly.

Jonathan shot the old man an angry look, trying to stop him from talking. "Look, mister, will you please not talk like that around my son?"

The old man seemed to hesitate for a moment and then understanding flooded his face and his countenance softened. "Oh, gees, you're right, I'm sorry, I don't know what I was thinking." Then he looked over at Billy. "Don't worry, there, sonny, your father's right. We'll be fine; you just wait and see."

Jonathan shifted his weight, climbing to his knees. "Listen, Billy, I need to put you down so I can see what happened, okay?"

Billy squeezed him tighter, not wanting to be let go.

"It's all right, I promise. I just want to see if I can get one of the doors open, maybe see if there are other people that need our help."

Billy hesitated for a second, but then he relaxed his arms.

"You're sure you're not gonna leave me?" Billy asked in his tiny voice.

Jonathan nodded. "Uh-huh, I'm not going anywhere."

Billy let him go and sat back on one of the canted seats. "Okay, Daddy, but be careful."

Jonathan grinned at his son. "You bet I will," he said and then turned to look at the old man. "Hey, if you're all right, want to help me with the doors?"

The man dusted off his lap and stood up with a grin. "Happy to help, whatever will get us out of here sooner rather than later, I'm all for it."

"You're both wasting your time," the woman said. "Just stay put until help arrives."

Slightly annoyed, Jonathan turned to look at her. The woman's face was barely discernable in the wan light of the emergency lamps. "Yes, well, thank you for your opinion again, but I think we'll be fine," Jonathan told her brusquely.

The woman only shrugged her shoulders and began digging into her purse, taking out a cell phone and trying to use it. What a shock when she found no signal.

In frustration, she tossed it back into the purse and dropped the bag onto the seat next to her, then she sat back and crossed her arms, deciding she would watch the show.

As for the bum, he merely sat on the seat he had climbed onto after hitting the floor and he watched everyone silently. No one talked to him.

Jonathan and the old man moved to the doors on the left side of the car and tried to open them, but the doors were sealed tight.

Jonathan put all of his muscle into opening it, his hands wrapped around the rubber gasket that lined the edge of each door, but nothing would budge.

After a full five minutes, he waved for them to stop. "Shit, they won't budge," he said to the old man.

"Told ya," the woman said briskly. Jonathan turned his head to glare at her, then decided what was the point.

That was when he heard something banging. "Hey, you hear that?" he asked the old man.

The man nodded, cocking his ear to the side.

"Yeah, I do. That's not mechanical. You can tell by the rhythm. That's got to be people."

"Come on, it's coming from the car in front of us," Jonathan said while moving back to the door he had slammed up against when the train had lurched to a halt.

The old man followed, and just before Jonathan reached the door, he took a moment to tussle his son's hair. Billy smiled up at him and giggled at the attention.

Jonathan got his hands on the door and yanked it open. The door opened with ease, sliding to the side, like a pocket door in a modern home.

Stepping over the small open area that separated the two cars from one another—only a small platform with large rubber walls that looked like the inside of an accordion on both sides—he opened the next door that would lead into the car in front of him.

Opening the door, he was shocked to see nothing but darkness, dust, and crushed metal.

"What the?" was all he could say. The emergency lights behind him weren't strong enough to penetrate into the next car, so he squinted his eyes a bit, trying to peer into the gloom.

Then the old man was next to him with a small Zippo lighter in his hand. Shoving the small flame forward, the lighter cast flickering shadows over the inside of the car, and they could see it was buried in rubble.

The roof of the car had collapsed under the weight of the tunnel ceiling and tons of rock and dirt had fallen inside the car, in all likelihood killing anyone who had been unfortunate enough to pick that car to ride in.

"Oh my Lord, there must have been a cave-in. That's what we felt before, and it looks like the front of the train is buried under a shitload of rocks and dirt," the old man said in shock.

"Then that means..." Jonathan said in a hushed voice.

The old man nodded. "Yeah, that everyone on the train in front of us is probably dead."

But then the banging sounded again and both men looked at one another.

"Daddy, are you okay?" Billy called from a few feet behind him.

"Yes, son, I'm fine, just stay there. I'll be back in a minute," Jonathan called.

"'Kay," Billy replied.

Turning back to the car in front of him, the old man had already entered it, climbing over some of the large boulders. He had only reached a few feet into the car when he called out to Jonathan.

"Over here, I've found someone!" he called out frantically. "Help me with this thing, will ya?"

Jonathan climbed over the rubble and helped the old man move the four foot piece of sheet metal that had fallen in from the roof. The work was hard and the air was growing stale, filled with dust.

The old man had jammed his lighter into a small outcropping of torn metal, and by the flickering light, the two men worked.

It was hot, sweaty work, but in ten minutes they managed to dislodge the piece of metal, shoving it off to the side. Jonathan looked down into a small hole to see a woman's dirty and frightened face looking up at him.

With eyes wide with terror, she reached out one shaking hand.

"Oh my God, thank God, I thought I was going to die under here. Please, help me," she said in a voice fraught with controlled panic.

Jonathan quickly scanned the area around her and made an educated guess. There didn't seem to be anything stopping the woman from just climbing up and out of the hole now that the roof piece was gone.

She was lucky. When the train had derailed, she had been tossed off her seat and had ended up rolling under the seats opposite her.

When the roof had fallen in, she had been saved by the seats above her, all hard plastic and metal with steel pipes running the length for support.

Jonathan reached down with his hand. "Here, take my hand and I'll pull you up," he told her.

"I don't know; there's something holding my leg. I can move it, but I don't know if it's free."

Jonathan smiled the same reassuring smile he had just used on his son at the woman and kept his voice as calm as he could, trying to sound confident. "Well, we'll just have to see then, won't we?"

She smiled back, though it wasn't heartfelt, her terror still in full force. Jonathan found himself impressed with this woman though he knew nothing about her.

She seemed strong and able to maintain a sense of calmness even though she was petrified inside. With his hand dangling over her head, the woman reached up and wrapped her hand around his.

"You got her?" the old man asked from his side.

"Yeah, I got her, you just keep the light on so I can see," Jonathan told him.

"You got it, chief," the old man replied.

Jonathan began pulling her up and out of the hole, his eyes locked on hers, waiting for her to cry out that her leg was in pain from whatever had grasped it, but she only nodded that she was fine.

"Your leg?" he asked, not happy with the fact that she was halfway out of the hole and doing fine when she said there was something holding her. He had heard stories of people in earthquakes and other tragedies that had thought their lower parts were all right until they were removed from the rubble to find the limb was missing altogether.

"It's okay. There's still something on it, but it's not holding me back. There was a slight tug when you pulled me the first time, but now it's fine."

"Okay, good, let me know if there's a problem," Jonathan said.

She only nodded, the gesture barely seen in the flickering light of the Zippo.

Another minute of gentle pulling found him leaning backward as she scrambled out of the hole of wreckage. By luck alone, the debris had landed in such a way that she had been spared the total impact of the crushed roof.

Overhead, where the ceiling of the car once was, the darkness of the tunnel couldn't be seen. The Zippo wasn't strong enough to penetrate it, but a few sparks shot out every few seconds, the severed wires making themselves known.

When the woman was entirely out of the hole, Jonathan stepped out of the way so she could stand up. There was almost no room from the wreckage to the door leading back to his car and he had to scurry back into the doorframe so she could fully stand up.

The old man had the Zippo in his hand again and he was moving it over the woman's body, checking for signs of wounds.

"I'm fine, really. I think I'd know if I was bleeding," she told him.

The old man shook his head. "Now, not so fast, there, missy, sometimes you can get some shrapnel in you and not even know it's there until infection sets in. Just hold still and let me check." He moved the lighter up and down her body and when he was inspecting her legs, he stopped and leaned back in surprise.

"What the hell...?" was all he said. "Hey, kiddo, come over here and see this," he told Jonathan.

Jonathan stepped over the rubble and leaned forward to see what was so interesting on the woman's leg. As he leaned in, the Zippo illuminated something long attached to her right ankle.

As the old man placed the Zippo on top of the object, the object became clear as day, and Jonathan let out a small gasp and leaped back, afraid it would grab him. Which was totally irrational. He just guessed he'd watched far too many zombie movies.

The old man chuckled at him and then told the woman to hold still.

She did as she was told and the old man fidgeted on her ankle for a second, then he stood back up with the object in his hand. "Here's what had a hold of you, young missy," he said with a slight sadness to his voice.

The woman turned to see what was attached to her and she gasped in shock, her right hand covering her mouth.

In the old man's left hand was a severed arm, the end that connected to the shoulder torn skin and material from the suit sleeve it was in and nothing but thin bits of gristle hanging from the edge.

As he held it in his hand, small drops of blood seeped from the end of the arm, and after he was sure everyone had seen it, he gently set it on top of the rubble.

"Holy shit, that's an arm. A human arm," Jonathan said in awe, his stomach rolling inside him.

The old man nodded. "Afraid so, must have been another rider who wasn't as lucky as you, miss," he said to the woman and made the sign of the cross. "Poor bastard, hope he's dead already."

"You mean he might not be?" Jonathan asked.

The old man shrugged, picking the arm up again and inspecting the end where it had been separated from its owner. "Depends; if the arm got pinched off when it came off then it's possible the wound might be sealed by the pressure of what's on top of the body. But chances are the guy bled out a few minutes after it happened; probably less." He sighed. "This is nothing. In the war I saw more body parts and dead bodies to last a hundred lifetimes. After you've been in the middle of that, well, this seems like a day at summer camp."

Jonathan stared at the severed arm and that was when he noticed the timepiece on the wrist. Though covered in blood, it was unmistakable. The arm had belonged to the man he had seen on the platform talking on his cell phone.

The old man shrugged and set the arm back down on top of the rubble.

"Why'd you do that? Seems a bit callous to just leave it there, doesn't it?" Jonathan asked.

"Why, did you need it?" the old man asked.

"Uh, well, I..." Jonathan stammered, not really having an answer. It just seemed like they should have held onto it--for evidence maybe.

"Do any of you know what happened to us?" the woman asked.

Jonathan and the old man stared at one another and then the woman.

"No, no idea, but hopefully help will be here soon to get us," Jonathan stated.

"Well, thanks for helping me. I don't know what I would have done if you hadn't come to my aid," she said to Jonathan and the old man, respectively.

Jonathan was struck by just how pretty she was. Even with her face and clothing covered in dust and dirt, she was very beautiful in a girl next door kind of way.

As he helped her closer to the doorway, he realized he had seen her on the platform. And now he, her, and the rest of them were trapped in a cave-in.

In a less than a half hour, all their perspectives on life had shifted.

The old man waited while the man and woman gazed at each other and then he cleared his throat.

When both pairs of eyes were looking at him, he gestured to the demolished car.

"It looks like we can try to climb out through the torn roof, but I think at this point that's a risky proposition."

"Why?" the woman asked.

The old man pointed to the exposed wires hanging down from the ceiling, most of them sparking fitfully.

"Because if one of us tries to get through there and something shifts, they're likely to end up getting electrocuted, that's why."

Jonathan stared up at the wires, contemplating what would happen if he tried to slide through one of the two small holes in the ceiling. The rest of the roof was gone, crushed by falling rocks and debris.

There would be no escaping that way anytime soon. Perhaps if the power was cut off, and even then, would the debris be stable enough to crawl over?

Or would it all shift and swallow the climber whole.

The old man waved for them to head back to their former car.

"Come on; let's get back to our car. At least there we can breathe easier," he said and stepped through the doorway. It was true, once they had passed through the door and had closed it behind them, the air was infinitely better, though a little murkier now thanks to the dust that had seeped through the open door.

The woman stepped into the car and immediately sat down on a seat. Billy was only three seats away from her and he watched her intently, almost like he was studying her.

The woman noticed after a few seconds that she was being watched and smiled at Billy. "Hello, there, what's your name?"

"I'm Billy," he said in a soft voice. His dad had always told him not to talk to strangers, but he had been scared waiting for his dad, and the other lady in the car and the dirty man who were with him had said nothing to him.

Jonathan sat down next to his son and hugged him. "This is my son, Billy, and I'm Jonathan, by the way."

"Oh, of course. You two saved me and I haven't even introduced myself."

She pointed to her chest with a dirty hand. "I'm Trudy, Trudy Harcourt."

Jonathan grinned her way. "Nice to meet you, Trudy." Then he looked over to the old man who had taken a seat across from him.

"How 'bout you, sir, what's your name?" Jonathan asked him.

The old man shrugged slightly, but in the pallid light from the emergency lights, it was hard to see the gesture.

"You can call me Eddie," he said flatly.

"All right, nice to meet you, Eddie," Jonathan said in return.

"Listen, if you guys are through with the introductions, then how 'bout we figure out what to do next." the woman in the power suit exclaimed from the opposite end of the car, now changing her tune and wanting to be part of the group. "Surely someone should have come by now," she finished.

Just then the door behind her was pushed open and people began flooding into the car with them along with small bits of rocks and debris.

Jonathan stood up, telling Billy to stay in his seat.

From the rear of the car, Jonathan saw the faces of the people he had seen boarding the train when they had pulled into the last stop before departing the station. Covered in dirt and dust, he saw the two teenagers stumble into the car, and behind them were the three Spanish people, the man and the two women.

He noticed now that they were closer to him, that each wore a blue jacket with their company's logo on it. He recognized the SSC as one of the many cleaning company's in the city. He had been right, they were building cleaners.

But it was the last man who entered that had Jonathan hoping for the best.

In the wan light, the T cop strode into the car. He was standing tall and his jaw was set tight. He was in total control of the situation, whatever the situation might be.

Holding his hands up in front of him, he tried to regain some order inside the car.

"All right, people, please stay calm. We had to come in here and join you because our car has collapsed in on itself. Luckily, we were all able to get to the front before it came down on our heads. It took us some time to clear the door, but here we are."

"Do you know what's going on, Officer?" Jonathan asked in a concerned voice, hoping the man did.

The cop moved through the aisle, gently shifting people to the side so he could pass. When he reached Jonathan, he looked down at him.

"I'm not really sure, sir, my radio's out, but it looks like there's been a cave-in."

"A cave-in? How the hell did that happen? For Christ's sake, this is Boston, not California!" Power Suit Woman yelled at him.

The cop took the abuse in stride, a professional to the end. He knew to keep everyone as calm as possible for as long as possible. At least until help arrived.

"Now, miss, just try to stay calm and everything will be fine. We just have to wait for a rescue crew to come dig us out. This has only happened one other time here and that was in the early 1900's; and I believe everyone got out of there alive."

"Well, sorry to break your record there, sonny, but there's at least one dead already," Eddie said while he gestured to the front of the car.

"Are you sure about that, sir? Maybe they just need help," the cop said, moving towards the doorway that would lead to the next car.

"No, sorry to say it, but we're pretty sure the guy's dead. But it's not like we know for sure. All we found was his severed arm," Jonathan told the cop.

The cop's right eyebrow went up in curiosity, but he said nothing, only grunting. Though he did stop moving towards the door.

"I'm sorry to hear that, but other than that I believe we're it. Can we get out through the next car?"

"No, the whole thing's caved in. There's a few small holes in the ceiling through the rubble, but they're surrounded by sparking wires," Jonathan told him.

"Hmm, what about this door, can we get it open?" the cop asked, moving to the double doors that would be used for passengers to exit the train onto the platforms at the stations. There was another set of double doors on the opposite side of the car, as well, but both doors were connected to the same hydraulics.

"Be my guest, sonny, but we already tried and the damn thing's closed tighter than a straight man's ass in prison. Must have frozen when the power cut off," Eddie told him.

The cop ignored the old man's warning and began trying to force the doors apart single-handedly. He did manage to pry the doors open two inches or so, but then they snapped shut again, only the rubber molding keeping him from losing some fingers. "Dammit," he spit, angrily.

"See, I told you so," Eddie said, sitting back in his seat. "Though I hate to admit it, the lady over there is probably right and we'll just have to wait for a rescue."

The cop was about to reply when a scraping sound filtered in from outside the car. It sounded like someone had an axe in their hands and was drawing it across the base of the train.

"Wait, did you hear that?" Jonathan asked excitedly.

For a moment no one heard him, everyone talking to themselves. The two teenagers were arguing with Power Suit Woman and the three cleaners were speaking Spanish to one another, arguing about something, or so Jonathan thought by the way they were waving their hands in the air at one another.

"Dammit, listen to me, there's someone outside on the tracks!" Jonathan yelled, and this time voices stopped, as everyone listened intently, looking at the walls of the car.

"Just listen, I know I heard something, it sounded like scraping," he said again, and pulled Billy closer to him.

Now all were silent, only the steady sound of each person's breathing filling the air. With everyone quiet, the sounds of rubble shifting and metal creaking could now be heard as the wrecked train settled under the weight of the collapsed tunnel.

At first there were no other sounds outside the car, the noise stopping. Power Suit Woman was about to speak when the scraping began again. Every single person in the car held their breath, listening to the scraping. The sound felt like someone was scratching their fingernails over a chalkboard, causing Jonathan's insides to tighten up.

His throat moved slightly as he swallowed, his Adam's apple bobbing up and down. Then the cop went into action, banging on the door, and trying to get the rescuer's attention.

"Hey! We're in here! Hello, we're in here!" the cop called out and soon other voices joined his. As for Jonathan, he sat in his seat, hugging Billy. Next to him, Trudy slid closer to him and he reached out his hand to her; which she took. Something wasn't right, though he had no idea what it could be.

If there were rescuers out on the tracks, then why didn't any of them inside the car hear the work crews as they shifted the rubble to enter the tunnel? And why weren't there any lights shining into the tunnel, as the work crews illuminated the danger zone.

But all these questions were in the back of his mind, nothing tangible he could put his finger on.

Soon, other passengers were banging on the dark windows of the train, hoping to get the attention of the work crews coming to save them.

The cop stood by the double doors, banging on them for help. In the middle of each door was a two foot long window, about a foot wide.

These were made of the same material as the windows lining the walls of the train and were just there so passengers could see the feet of other people when the train would pull up at a brightly lit platform.

Jonathan sat in his seat, watching the cop bang on the door. The cop turned around then, as if he was going to say something to Jonathan, and right before Jonathan's eyes, like the flash of a camera going off, the left window on the door shattered, sending black crystals of tempered glass flying everywhere.

Jonathan looked away for a moment, protecting his eyes on instinct, his other hand covering Billy's face, and when he looked up again, the cop was screaming.

Like trying to shove a square peg into a round hole, the cop was being pulled through the small window by his waist.

In the shadows of the emergency lights, Jonathan could only see the briefest glimpse of claw-like hands wrapped around the cop's torso. The hands were yanking him backward, through the small hole, and the cop was far too large to fit.

With his mouth hanging open in shock, Jonathan watched the cop bend at the waist, like he was being folded, and then his ass was pulled into the broken window.

Screaming for help, blood shooting out of the cop's mouth like a geyser as his internal organs ruptured and compacted, his body was slowly pulled through the window inch by agonizing inch.

The man was bent over, his head in-between his knees as he was yanked through the hole bit by bit.

That was when Jonathan broke free of his stupor, handed Billy to Trudy roughly, and lunged across the car, his right hand out to grab the cop's left hand. At the same time, one of the cleaners, the older man with a mustache, did the same thing, grabbing the cop's right hand.

With Jonathan and the cleaner holding on, they each tried to pull the cop back through the window.

A scarlet jet of blood shot out of the cop's mouth again, bathing the cleaner in gore, and the man's grasp slipped as he shied away.

"Please...don't let...go..." the cop choked through blood, his face so red it looked like it was about to explode like a massive red pimple.

Even with the other passengers screaming and yelling from the sight of the man being yanked through the window, Jonathan could hear the popping and snapping of the cop's bones as he was slowly pulled further and further out of the train.

Jonathan struggled to hold on, but even as he was slowly pulled toward the window, he watched the light go out of the man's eyes. The cop's head slumped down as the massive trauma to his chest and heart finally reached its conclusion and he died.

Jonathan let go, and just as he did, there was one more mighty tug at the body and the cop slid through the window to be lost in the darkness.

Running to the broken window, Jonathan looked out into the tunnel. It was almost pitch black, but the sparking wires would flash every so often, resembling lightning on a storm-tossed night.

He saw the cop's feet being dragged across the ground and he tried to see what had a hold of him, but all he could see were black shapes that seemed to blend into the darkness like chameleons.

Then the cop was gone from view and there was nothing to see. But there were sounds to hear. Cocking his head to the side, Jonathan could hear the sounds of feeding, of bones snapping and flesh being torn, though it was hard to know for sure, as the other passengers inside the car were freaking out, his son included.

Stepping away from the window, he ran to Billy, scooping him up in his arms and hugging him close; Trudy passing the boy to him easily.

"What the hell just happened, man? What the hell just happened?" the cleaner covered in blood asked, his accent heavy but easy to understand. "What the hell could do that to a man?"

Eddie was up as well, staring out the broken window.

"Jesus Christ, what the hell just happened here?" he whispered, his eyes never leaving the broken window. Around the edge of the window, blood dripped, vermilion rivulets that slid down the door to pool on the silver molding where the door met the floor.

"There's nothing alive that I know of that could do that, especially down here in the tunnels," Eddie said, taking a step back from the window. "This can't be real, it just can't."

"Oh my God, we're all gonna die down here. We're all gonna die!" Power Suit Woman yelled, wringing her hands in front of her in terror as she stared at the broken window.

It was Trudy who dealt with Power Suit Woman, walking over to her and slapping her across the face, the resounding slap echoing inside the car. Power Suit Woman looked up at Trudy, eyes wide with fear, but she stopped screaming, bringing her hand up to her face to touch where she'd been slapped. In the dull light of the car, a small red mark could be seen on her cheek. After that, a few of the others quieted down, also.

"Dammit, listen to me," Trudy said. "We have to stay calm. I don't know what's happening here, either, but whatever it is, we're not going to do anything about it by freaking out!"

Jonathan stood up then, Billy still in his arms.

"She's right," he said. "We need to stay focused. Find a way out of here and then escape the tunnel."

"But what about the cop, man? What about the fucking cop? Whatever just did that to him is out there? It could be waiting for us," the cleaner ranted while wiping blood from his face with a wrinkled handkerchief.

"That's true," Eddie said, now joining the conversation. The entire time the cop had been yanked through the door, he had merely stared, open-mouthed. "But it's probably just some crazy homeless guy that lives in the tunnel. After the cave-in, he must have freaked out and attacked the cop."

Jonathan gave that idea some thought for a moment. He decided not to say anything about the claws he'd seen, or thought he'd seen. To tell the truth, now that it was all over, he wondered if maybe he had just imagined it all and Eddie was right.

Hell, it would sure make a lot more sense, he reasoned. After all, what would be the alternative? Some kind of C.H.U.D.-like creatures running around the subway tunnels of Boston?

Ridiculous.

"Are you insane, old man? Whatever pulled that cop through the door sure as hell wasn't human. No way could a human being do that," the cleaner said, his voice filled with panic. "Unless the guy was high on PCP or smack or something."

Jonathan watched him talk, and as the man stepped under one of the emergency lights, he saw the name **Carlos** stitched on the left breast of his jacket.

"Look, Carlos," Jonathan said, trying to reason with the man. "Whatever we saw, it had to be a man. This is Boston for Christ's sake, not the Twilight Zone."

Carlos turned to stare at Jonathan. "Look, man, I don't really care what any of you people say. I know what I just saw. Ever hear of El Chupacabra? Well, I guess you got them here too. You just don't want to believe it."

Trudy turned to Jonathan. "El Chupacabra? What's that? It does sound familiar."

Eddie spoke up then. "It's a folk tale about monsters on the countryside. Mexican or Spanish I think. There's supposed to be this vampire-like creature that kills cows and sucks their blood. It's all a story to scare children into being good."

Carlos was talking to the other two people that were with him, the man and the woman. Jonathan figured out pretty quick that these two people didn't know English very well as Carlos was filling them in using Spanish on the topic of conversation presently being discussed. The woman answered back and Jonathan definitely heard El Chupacabra in her words, though he didn't understand much else.

Finally Carlos turned back to the others, his face set. "There, you see? Roselle agrees with me."

"What about the other guy? What does he say?" Eddie asked.

Carlos asked a few questions to the other man, and after a minute, Carlos turned back to Eddie. "Caesar doesn't have an opinion. He says it can't be true, but then what the hell just happened? He's willing to go with whatever decision the rest of us make. He's like that, easy going to the point it gets ridiculous."

At the sound of his name, Caesar nodded happily, as if he knew what Carlos was saying about him and agreed with all of it.

There was the sound of someone clearing his throat, followed by the sound of someone hawking up phlegm, followed by a spitting sound.

All eyes turned to see the man sitting by the rear door of the car. It was the bum. The entire time he had said nothing, just watching what everyone did and said. Now he spoke up, and as Jonathan stared at him, he saw a man that didn't look like he was all there.

"You people are all full of shit, you know that? I've been listening to you all talking back and forth and I can't take it anymore. Listen to me, all of you. I've lived in and around the subway for over ten years and I've seen some strange shit. The shit you won't hear about on the evening news. Some of the other guys I used to know went down into the lowest tunnels to stay warm in the winter, and come spring, no one ever saw them again. Sometimes there's been stories about people seeing these *things*. They look like us, but they're off, you know? They got long fingers like claws and their skin is all dark, so they can blend into the darkness. That's what happened to the cop. When the roof collapsed, it must have woke some of them up. It happens sometimes, but not too often."

For a few heartbeats, no one said a word, but merely stared at the bum.

Then Eddie barked laughter and sat down. "Are you serious, buddy? Monsters living in the tunnels? Come on, that's crazy. If there was such a thing, then wouldn't we have heard about it by now?"

The bum took two steps toward Eddie, his index finger pointing at him accusingly. "Why the hell would you? It's not like anyone listens to me or my kind. And the transit cops and workers never go down that deep. Even if they do, they have lights and shit with them which gives the things more than enough time to hide."

Eddie crossed his legs and leaned back, checking his wristwatch like he had a date. "I don't care what you say, it's all crazy and I won't hear anymore of it. It was just some bum, like you, probably. And now you're trying to cover it up for the bastard. Look, I changed my mind about what I said before. Let's just wait here until help arrives. I don't want to be running around out there if there's some crazy homeless people waiting for us to come out so they can rob us and God knows what else."

The bum was about to refute the accusation when Jonathan decided it was time to step in. "All right, listen, enough, please," Jonathan pleaded. "You're scaring my son. Whatever happened will all get sorted out when help arrives. Until then, I think we should all just sit down and stay put."

"But what about if that man who took the policeman comes back? What do we do then?" Power Suit Woman asked with fear in her eyes.

Eddie was the one to answer. "Listen up, everybody, just stay away from the doors and sit down. Jonathan, let's see if we can get some pipes or something to use as weapons...just in case."

Jonathan nodded and handed Billy to Trudy. "Will you hold him for me while I go with Eddie?" he asked her.

"Sure, Jonathan, no problem," Trudy said with a warm smile. "Come here, honey, and sit with me. I need someone to keep me company."

Billy consented and Jonathan moved away from his son, Eddie already up and ready to go into the front car where they had found Trudy. As soon as the two men stepped through the doorway into the next car, the sounds of discontent floated to their ears behind them.

Jonathan took note of this with Eddie. "You know, Eddie, we've got a lot of different people with different ideas on what's right and wrong. You know that, right? We'll never get them to agree with one another," he said as he began poking around in the rubble for some kind of a weapon. "It's like the damn United Nations in there."

Next to him, his hands digging and tossing wreckage aside, Eddie chuckled. "Yeah, or they're like Congress. They need to discuss something for days when all someone needs is to just say yes or no. What we need is someone to take charge, like that cop was doing before he got taken."

"That's not a bad idea, actually, Eddie. And I think it should be you."

Eddie stopped digging and looked up, trying to see Jonathan in the dark.

"Me? You want me to lead? I'm just an old man. No one listens to me anymore."

"Well, I would. Look, obviously you've seen some shit that the rest of us can only imagine. The closest I've ever come to a war is what I see on CNN. You're perfect for the job. So what do you say?"

Eddie began rooting through the wreckage again, and a moment later he yanked a pipe from a large pile near the edge of the car.

If Eddie was going to answer Jonathan, the answer would have to wait, because when Eddie removed the pipe, the entire pile shifted and some rubble and bits of stone fell to roll away onto the floor.

Both men shifted to the side, not wanting to get their feet crushed, and that was when the rest of the business man's body was found.

At first, the dead man was nothing but a shadow amidst other shadows, but then Eddie pulled out his Zippo and flicked the small wheel, igniting the flame.

Holding the lighter down to the floor, both men gazed down at what had, less than an hour ago, been a living breathing human being, with hopes and dreams and emotions and all the other wonderful things that made each one of God's creations beautiful.

But now all that lay on the floor, buried under hundreds of pounds of rubble, was a husk, an empty shell, surrounded by congealing blood.

Eddie moved the lighter closer, the flame flickering gently.

"Do you think he's dead?" Jonathan asked.

"Well, shit, yeah, he's dead," Eddie said, moving the Zippo to the right side of the corpse's head. When the light illuminated the man's head, it was blatantly apparent he was most definitely deceased.

The right side of his head had been pulverized by the pressure and weight of the rubble that had landed on him, not to mention all the blood. The man was only visible from the shoulders down and it was now easy to see where the man's arm had been severed from his torso.

It was a gruesome sight, made even more horrifying in the shadows of the flickering Zippo, as the blood reflected the light like a dull mirror.

"Poor bastard," Eddie said, reaching out and closing the man's remaining eye.

Jonathan crossed himself, old habits hard to break, and then he reached out, picked up a small piece of sheet metal and laid it over the dead man's face.

"Rest in piece, fella," he said quietly.

"Amen," Eddie said softly.

Just before the two men turned away, Jonathan heard a soft beeping. "Hey, Eddie, wait a second. You hear something?"

Eddie shook his head no and pointed to his ears. "A grenade went off too close to me in the war. Don't hear much if it ain't right in front of my face. Why, you hear somethin'?"

Jonathan nodded and went to one knee, cocking his head to listen. It was hard, trying to focus while the passengers in the next car continued arguing.

"Hey, Eddie, close that door, will ya? I can't hear too well."

Deciding to humor the young man, Eddie did as he was asked, sliding the door closed with a soft click.

The moment the door closed, Jonathan's ears picked up the beeping better, now able to zero in on it. Moving around slowly, he ended up over the corpse again.

Removing the sheet metal, feeling like he was desecrating a grave, he put his head as close as he could to the man's crushed skull. As he leaned over him, the odors of after shave, blood and dirt came to his nose, making him want to sneeze, or throw-up, or both simultaneously.

He heard the soft beeping again, he reached down, and shifted the man's body. As soon as he did this, the beeping grew louder.

There was a small light showing now and Jonathan stretched out and retrieved the cell phone that had become trapped under the man's body when he had fallen to the floor, and been subsequently crushed.

The man's body had protected the phone from being destroyed and Jonathan stood up with the prize in his hand, waving it back and forth so Eddie could see it.

"Hot damn, a phone," Eddie said happily. "Great job, son. Call someone and get us the hell out of here."

Jonathan held the phone to his eyes and immediately saw there was no signal, no bars. Holding the phone over his head and waving it around like a bad cell phone commercial, he was still rewarded with nothing.

"Dammit, there's no signal down here. There's probably thousands of tons of rock and earth over our heads. This damn thing is useless."

He was going to toss it back onto the pile, but realized the small screen was a paltry light but still better than nothing, so he put it into his pocket for safe keeping.

Dejected but still optimistic, Eddie patted him on the shoulder. "That's okay, son, it was worth a try."

Eddie bent over and handed Jonathan a two-foot piece of rebar, keeping the pipe he'd found for himself. "Here, take this, it'll do the job if one of those tunnel bastards tries to get in here again."

Jonathan took the rebar in silence and turned to leave the car, Eddie right behind him. Just before Eddie was going to walk into the car, he paused and stepped back to the corpse.

Picking up the severed arm, he rested it on the man's back, picked up the piece of sheet metal, holding it carefully in his hands so as not to become cut from the serrated edges, and placed it back over the man's head and shoulders. Then he followed Jonathan back into the main car.

When Eddie had stepped through the doorway, and had pulled it closed behind him, the soft click of the latch was the only sound in the destroyed car.

But soon the sounds of scurrying and scratching could be heard coming from around the body.

A second later, rubble began to shift and the sheet metal over the corpse's head shifted and fell to the floor with a muffled *clang* as the body began to be pulled backward into the rubble, one inch at a time.

A bloody trail of bone and brain matter was left on the floor as the body was slowly pulled into the wreckage.

Then, with one quick yank, the body slid from view, the remaining arm and hand trailing after the corpse like it was reaching out for help.

The severed arm fell off the body to tumble to the floor, where it remained for a second or two, until a black claw reached out and grabbed it, so fast that if someone was watching and blinked, they would have missed the action.

When the scuttling had stopped and the body had completely disappeared from under the rubble, the hole that had been formed around the body fell in on itself, filling the area the dead man's husk had been in only moments before.

The sound of a trap door, a service door, actually, that each car had in the floors that led to the underside of each car, slammed shut again, and the sounds of scratching and scuttling could be heard outside on the gravel of the tunnel floor.

Then silence regained its foothold inside the demolished car, the only other sounds now coming from the final car that still had living humans inside.

Jonathan stepped into the car and frowned as he watched the passengers arguing with one another. Caesar and Roselle were going at it in Spanish, the bum was arguing with Carlos, and Power Suit Woman was arguing with the two teenagers who seemed to have gotten their voices back.

It was loud and annoying and finally, Jonathan couldn't take it anymore. "Enough!" he screamed, smacking his piece of rebar against the wall of the train, the loud *whack* causing everyone to look his way and stop talking like a switch had been flicked. "What the hell is wrong with you people? Look, I don't know what's going on anymore than you do, but arguing about it isn't going to accomplish a damn thing. Listen up, I'm making a rule right now. Anyone who wants to work together and deal with this crazy situation come over here and stand with me and Eddie. The rest of you can stay over there and shut the fuck up. Well, what's it gonna be?"

No one moved, paralyzed by the rage in Jonathan's voice and the piece of rebar he held in his hand, which he had been waving around menacingly, not realizing it.

Trudy stood up, and though she was only a few feet away from him, she moved the few feet so she was standing next to him. As she did this, she handed Billy to him, who hugged his father with tears in his eyes.

Jonathan could feel his son's heart beating in his small chest as his body pressed against his and it made him want to cry. He never wanted his son to have to experience the fear and confusion he was feeling right now.

"I'm with you, Jonathan, just say what we should do," Trudy said with a smile.

Jonathan nodded to her, smiling as well. Looking into her eyes, he felt something he hadn't felt since his wife had died.

Was it hope? Hope that he could care for another woman again?

Eddie clapped his hands together as he glared at the other passengers.

"Well? What's it gonna be, folks? Are you with us or against us?"

Carlos held up a finger for him to wait and then he spoke rapidly in Spanish, filling in Caesar and Roselle on what had just occurred.

Both replied and then began talking to themselves, the entire conversation taking less than a minute. Then, with Caesar going first, the three of them crossed the car to join Jonathan and the others.

"Good, that's great, glad to have you with us," Jonathan said to Carlos, shaking the man's hand.

"No problema, amigo" Carlos said and then realized Jonathan might not understand. "Oh, sorry, I said no problem, we're with you. It is as good as anything else and better than fighting amongst ourselves."

Caesar nodded, smiling widely, as if he was part of the conversation.

"That's great," Jonathan said, then turned to look at the others. "How 'bout the rest of you? You in or out?"

The two teenagers looked at one another and then the first one shrugged and said, "Yeah, man, it's cool, we're with you. We just want to get out of here in one piece."

The second teenager agreed with his friend and the two crossed the car, standing next to the three cleaners.

"That's great, guys. Say, you two got names?" Jonathan asked.

"Yeah, man, I'm Glen and he's Chris," the first teenager said.

"Okay, good, Glen and Chris, good to know you," Jonathan said, shifting Billy on his arm. God how heavy he was getting.

There were only two more people left at the end of the car: the bum and Power Suit Woman.

"Well, what about you two?" Jonathan asked them as amiably as he could muster under the circumstances.

The bum made a sound, like a raspberry, and he shot his middle finger at Jonathan and the others. "Fuck you, I don't need any of you, I've been surviving in these tunnels for years and I'll be around years after you're all worm food."

Jonathan frowned, not exactly happy with being cursed at and insulted, but instead of replying, he turned to look at Power Suit Woman.

"Well, miss, what about you?" he asked.

All eyes in the car turned and stared at the woman. She sat in her seat, high-heels and pant suit that showed off her shapely legs. Her suit was dusty, but she had done her best to wipe it clean.

She was staring back at everyone as they waited for her answer, when the floor seemed to explode upwards under her feet. She screamed and jumped onto her seat, like she had seen a mouse, and that simple act saved her life.

As the service door in the floor popped open, claw-like hands reached out from under the train; searching for prey. In the emergency lights of the car, it was difficult to see anything clearly, and as soon as the hatch popped open, everyone began screaming and trying to do something, anything, whether it was to escape or attack the threat.

But it was the bum who had the unfortunate luck of standing directly next to the hatch. Before he could so much as shriek, scream or curse, he was yanked off his feet by the ankles and pulled into the hatch.

In less than five seconds, the hatch had popped open, the bum had been pulled into the dark hole, and the hatch was closed again.

Though everyone tried to help the bum, by the time Jonathan had given Billy to Trudy, and Eddie and him had tried to fight their way through the other passengers—though Carlos did join in the battle with what was in the hatch—the entire episode was over, leaving everyone within the train filled with a sense of hollowness. Adrenalin was pumping and there was nothing to fight.

Jonathan ran to the double doors where the cop had been pulled through, and just as he gazed out into the darkness through the broken window, he saw the bum's face.

The man appeared to be floating about four feet above the ground, though the sense of dark shadows under him was prevalent.

His face was one of surprise, and his mouth was hanging open, his lips moving up and down as if he was trying to say something.

From Jonathan's vantage point inside the train, he couldn't see that the bum's throat had been slashed by a razor-like claw and all Jonathan could hear was the man's death rattle.

Then the bum was lost in the darkness and all was peaceful outside the train.

Inside the car, it was chaos as everyone tried to talk at once and Power Suit Woman cried steadily. Billy had begun crying as well. Though he didn't know why, he could sense the dread inside the car and for him it was nothing but fear.

Trudy consoled him, standing against the front door of the car, watching the floor with wide eyes of terror, expecting it to burst open again at any second.

Jonathan turned back to the others. Eddie was at the closed hatch and said, "It's some kind of service opening. For the maintenance crew probably."

"How are we going to stop it from opening again? And what the hell grabbed that guy? I saw something and it sure didn't look like any hands I ever saw before," Carlos ranted, his face a mask of panic.

Jonathan let out a heavy breath and tried to slow his beating heart. Whatever had just happened, it was over now, and for the moment, they were safe again, though for how long that might be was anyone's guess.

"Look, we need to have people stand on the hatch. That way, they, whatever they are, can't push it open. And we need to make sure there aren't any other hatches in this car. If there are, they could just go through those later and pick us off one by one."

"Good idea, Jonathan," Eddie said, and began inspecting the rest of the floor. "Carlos, have Caesar or Roselle stand on the hatch so it doesn't open again," Jonathan told him.

"Si, Senor," Carlos said, speaking to Caesar and Roselle quickly, telling them what needed to be done. As soon as he had explained it, both man and woman did as asked, crossing the car and stomping down hard on the hatch with their feet, where they remained.

Next to them, Power Suit Woman cried into her blouse, her eyes staring at nothing.

A minute later, Eddie returned to Jonathan's side.

"The place looks okay. If there are anymore hatches in here, I can't find them.

"Good, that's good," Jonathan said.

Eddie was grinning, and for the life of him, Jonathan had no idea why the old man would be doing that, as they were all in mortal danger.

"Why the hell are you smiling?" Jonathan asked, curiously.

"Because we found our leader, guess you didn't know you had it in you, huh?"

Jonathan shrugged. "No, I guess not, well okay then, if I'm in charge, here's what we need to do." He held up his hand and began ticking off fingers as he counted. "One, we need to post a watch on that broken window as well as the other doorways. Two, we need to figure out what our next move is going to be. Is it, A, wait here for help to arrive, or B, try to get out into the tunnel and try to dig our way out. For all we know, there's a way out and all we have to do is get to it."

"I'll do whatever you think is best, Jonathan, just say the word," Trudy said from the seat next to him. Though she tried to look courageous, it was clear in her eyes she was petrified.

Carlos walked back to the middle of the car and turned to look at Jonathan.

"My vote is for getting out of here. Those things are picking us off one at a time. We need to just make a run for it. If we all fight, then we should make it."

"Easy for you to say, dude, but what if it's not you that freak out there goes for next?" Glen asked by the rear door. He kept looking back into the car he had come from, as if he was looking for something.

Carlos turned to face the teenager. "Well, if we stay here, what happens then? We've been here for almost an hour already and nobody's come to rescue us. Why the hell not? Surely someone knows there was a cave-in."

Eddie frowned. "Yeah, I've been thinking about that and I don't think you'll like what I've come up with. The T has been doing cutbacks big time. It's very possible there was no one in the switching room at the time the tunnel collapsed. It's possible everyone has already gone home. Chances are they left a half hour before the tunnel fell in. Once the driver got back to the yard, he probably just went home. It's very possible no one will know we're down here until five, maybe six in the morning."

"But that means it could be over four hours before anyone knows we're down here," Jonathan said. "And after that it's still gonna take time to get a rescue crew together and dig us out. That could add even more hours; two or three at least."

"Yeah, I know. That doesn't bode too well for us, I'm afraid," Eddie stated.

"Daddy, when are we gonna go home? I'm tired and hungry and I want to go to bed," Billy said from the seat next to Trudy as he rubbed his eyes.

Jonathan smiled down at his son, trying to be strong. "I know, buddy, but I think we're gonna be here for a little while longer. I'm sorry."

Trudy's eyes lit up and she reached into her pocket and pulled out half a candy bar. "Hey, Billy, do you want to finish this for me?" she asked with a smile.

Billy looked to Jonathan, who nodded yes. "Sure, go ahead and take it."

Billy did, and a second later was chewing happily.

Trudy wiped Billy's hair off his forehead and watched him eating. "And when you're done with that, you can stretch out on the seats and use my lap for a pillow. How's that sound?" she asked.

Billy only nodded, concentrating on his candy bar.

Jonathan smiled at Trudy and whispered a thank you. She returned the smile and reached out her hand for him. He took it and squeezed her hand once, then she took it away.

For just a brief flash of clarity, he realized in the midst of all the craziness and death he was falling for this woman who had taken to his son like a mother bear to her cubs. Then he had to focus on the here and now as Carlos was speaking.

"So I think we should try and make a run for it," Carlos finished, Jonathan missing the first half, though he knew what he missed was just a repeat of what Carlos had said before.

"Look, Carlos, you might be right," Jonathan said. "But what if you're not? We should hold up here for a while and see what happens. Tell you what; if nothing happens in two hours, then we'll try it your way. By then we won't have a choice."

Carlos bit his lip as he mulled it over and then nodded and said, "Okay, Jonathan, fine, we'll do it your way. For now."

Jonathan nodded as well. "For now," he repeated. "Now, why don't we all just rest up and try to relax. Who's gonna watch the broken window?"

Eddie spoke up. "Yeah, I've been thinking about that. Why don't we see if we can get a piece of metal or something from one of the other cars and use it as a cover for the window. That way someone can just lean against it."

"That's a good idea, Eddie," Jonathan said. "Any volunteers to go on a hunt?"

Chris held up his hand. "We'll go, I need to see if I can find my guitar in all that shit back there," he gestured to the caved in car he had vacated.

"Okay, here, take this with you," Jonathan said, passing the re-bar he'd been holding. "It's better than nothing."

Chris took the bar and nodded thanks. "Cool, thanks. Okay, we'll be right back."

"Good luck, son," Eddie said to the teenager.

Chris waved a thank you and then the two boys were opening the door and stepping out of the emergency lights. As for the rest of the weary passengers, they all sat down to rest.

Caesar and Roselle merely sat on the floor, their butts on the hatch, while Power Suit Woman cried softly. She had totally lost it. A child of the twentieth century, she wasn't able to handle hardship or discomfort.

Jonathan sat next to Billy; Trudy on his son's other side.

With the boy sandwiched between them, he stretched out and tried to sleep.

Eddie sat across from the broken window, the pipe in his hands. His jaw was set and his eyes clear. Like in the war, he took his post as a guard very seriously. Nothing would get past him without having to deal with him first.

The two teenagers could be heard digging around in the next car and Jonathan was wondering if he should go and keep an eye on them, but the truth was, he was exhausted.

Though only an hour had passed since the tunnel had collapsed, it felt like he had been inside the train for more than a day.

He was hungry, also, not to mention thirsty, and he wasn't looking forward to the next few hours where the thirst would only grow.

Not to mention his son. He was young and didn't understand he would have to wait. In his pampered life, when he was hungry or thirsty, he got what he wanted, immediate gratification for his needs.

Now, inside the train, trapped by a cave-in and something that surely had to be human, though crazy, he would not be getting what he wanted, and perhaps, what he needed. All he could do was try to make his son's discomfort less, and hope for the best, though it broke his heart to do so.

And it would be a lot longer than a few hours before the situation became dire, in the food and water category anyway. He still couldn't wrap his head around everything that had happened so far.

He'd been to busy acting to actually think about the truly ridiculous situation he and the other passengers now found themselves in.

The tunnel collapse was bad enough, but crazy homeless people that were attacking them like animals? It was ridiculous. It was fodder for some cheesy B movie with a bad plot and even worse actors.

But if that were true, then how could he explain away what had happened to the T cop? That man had been yanked through that small window like he was made of clay.

The sheer amount of strength to do that would surely surpass a human male, even more than one. And what about the blur that had taken the bum? That occurred so fast he still couldn't believe it actually happened.

No, whatever was going on outside in the tunnel, he doubted it would be a pleasant explanation when it was all over and they were rescued.

A cheer rang out from the next car, as one of the teenagers called out that he found his guitar. But then he cursed when he yelled that it was destroyed, the case not strong enough to protect the instrument inside.

There was some more rummaging and shifting of rocks from the car, but Jonathan ignored it, truly beginning to relax. His heart was finally slowing as he tried to make sense of everything he'd experienced thus far.

Trudy smiled wanly at him as she rubbed Billy's shoulder soothingly. "He really is a special boy, you know that?"

"Yeah, I know. When my wife died, he was the only thing keeping me going," Jonathan told her sadly.

She appeared embarrassed and she looked away from him, her eyes studying one of the posters on the wall, though in the dim light, she was probably just looking for an excuse to look away from him.

"Oh, I didn't know, I'm so sorry for you...and Billy," she said softly.

He forced a smile at her, though it wasn't real this time. It was just something he did when someone told him how sorry they were for his loss. It was a way to put them at ease so they didn't feel pity for him.

"That's all right. It's been almost a year now and I think I'm finally coming to grips with it."

She nodded. "Oh, that's good. I'm glad."

"What about you? Married? Boyfriend?" he asked, trying to change the subject.

"Me? Oh God, no. I mean, I've dated, but I never seem to find the right guy...at least not yet."

He smiled at her again, and this time it was genuine. "Don't worry, I'm sure you'll find someone, it just takes time," he said out loud, but inside he wanted to say, *And maybe that guy is me.*

She smiled back, and for the first time since he had met her, he didn't need to talk to keep the silence at bay.

He looked into her eyes and she into his. And with Billy laying between them with his head on her lap, for some reason, everything seemed right. Just for that one brief instant.

Then the moment was shattered by screams of pain coming from the two teenagers in the next car.

Jonathan looked up, prepared to go see what was wrong when a black shape appeared in the open doorway that separated the two cars from one another.

The creature hissed at the passengers and held up its right claw. Hanging from the claw was the severed head of Glen, the face still frozen in shock at the moment his head was separated from his shoulders.

But it was the eyes that were the most appalling; or lack thereof. The eyes were missing, the empty, bloody sockets dripping blood onto the head's cheeks in small rivulets, like scarlet tears. But the eyes weren't exactly missing.

They were in the creature's other hand, and like it was holding a pair of hardboiled eggs, the creature popped the eyes into its mouth, chewing heartily.

Before anyone could react, the creature tossed the head into the main car, blood droplets spraying from the jagged neck, the head rolling across the floor like a warped bowling ball until it stopped at Eddie's left foot, who was gazing down at it in shock.

Jonathan stared at the black shape in absolute terror, not knowing what to do for a precious second.

He was like a deer caught in the headlights of an oncoming vehicle on a lonely road in the country. Then, as if things couldn't get any worse, the emergency lights flicked off inside the car, plunging the train into utter darkness.

With everyone screaming and trying to figure out what to do next, the black creature charged out of the doorway, directly into the group of passengers.

Then total chaos ruled the darkness as each person fought for their life.

Jonathan jumped up from his seat but was immediately knocked back down by someone, though who it might have been was unknown in the utter darkness of the car.

"Trudy, get on the floor and under the seats with Billy!" Jonathan yelled at her, feeling for her shoulder and shoving her to the floor. He didn't know if she did as instructed, because an instant later, he was hit hard by a body, his face becoming squashed in the folds of its clothing.

He smelled Old Spice and sweat as the body fell on top of him and he struggled to keep his face from getting buried under the body's clothing, worried he might not be able to breathe. He shoved as hard as he could with his arms, and then he was breathing freely again; the body falling away from him with flailing arms and legs.

His ears were filled with screaming and shrieking as everyone tried to get away from the creature now in their midst.

Another body struck him, causing him to fall, and his head hit the floor hard, his vision showing white flashes of light like small stars.

Shaking his head, he thought he heard his son crying and tried to reach out and find him, but in the darkness he could see nothing. Then a foot landed on his right hand and he cried out, yanking the hurt hand to his chest and crawling away from what he perceived as danger.

Another scream and a squeal came to his ears as someone else was hurt. In the darkness of the car, it was impossible to know who it was. Then he could hear Eddie's voice yelling over the chaos. "Everyone, get to the front of the car! Now!" the old man yelled, though why he wanted everyone to do this was unknown. Jonathan was already at the front of the car, and a second later he felt a few more bodies surrounding him.

He could hear people speaking Spanish above him and he knew it must be Roselle, Carlos and Caesar. Then he heard a woman cry out and he was pretty sure it was Power Suit Woman. That was when he realized he had never learned the woman's name.

He could hear Eddie grunting and the sound of metal striking metal. Glass shattered and the tinkling sound filtered into the car and over the yelling people as they all tried to get to the front of the car and away from danger.

Jonathan tried to get off the floor, managing to pull himself onto a seat. He was petrified. He had no weapon and it was pitch black. Just how the hell was he, or anyone else, supposed to fight the thing that had entered the car with them?

Eddie grunted again and there was the sound of metal striking meat, a dull thump that was felt more than heard.

Then there was the scratching of claws, or long toenails, on the floor of the car, followed by a high-pitched scream that squelched all other sound. It was so high and loud that Jonathan was pretty sure it didn't come from one of the passengers.

Suddenly, all the noise around him seemed to quiet down, only the frightened whimpers and crying of the other passengers filling the train car.

"Eddie? Are you there?" Jonathan called out.

In heavy gasping breaths, Eddie answered, "Yeah, I'm still here, Jonathan. And I think I scared the bastard off. Here, wait a second. Just let me get my..."

There was a spark and a small light lit up the middle of the car. Eddie stood there, the metal pipe he had found in his left hand and his Zippo in his right. God, how Jonathan loved that Zippo. If it wasn't for that lighter, what would any of them have done?

Jonathan moved off his seat, his eyes already searching for his son. He was praying in his head that Billy was all right, and a moment later, he saw him, wrapped in Trudy's arms under a row of seats, both of them curled up tight.

There was a foot and a half of space from the floor to the bottom of the seats and Trudy and Billy had fit inside easily.

Reaching down, he took Billy from her arms and helped her out.

"Is it safe? Are we okay?" Trudy asked, her eyes wide with fright.

"Yeah, honey, I think we're okay," Eddie said to her. The car wasn't that large and he heard her question easily. "I'm pretty sure I got a few good licks in. I think I scared it off."

Jonathan held Billy with his right arm and pulled Trudy next to him with his left.

"Hey, kiddo, how you doin'?" Jonathan asked Billy.

His son was in tears again, his face drawn and tired and frightened and a dozen other emotions, all crossing his face at the same time. "I'm scared, Daddy, I don't want to be here anymore. Can we leave now, please?" he begged, his head going against Jonathan's chest as he tried to burrow under his father's arm for safety.

"I know, Billy, God I know. You just have to hang in there a little longer."

Jonathan rubbed Billy's back, trying to comfort him. He truly believed he would give his life up right now, at this exact second, if it would see his son safely out of the Hell he'd been thrown into.

Then he looked over to Eddie. "What the hell was that thing?" he asked, his shaking voice evident to all, not that any of the others noticed or cared. They all felt the exact same way.

Eddie shook his head. "I don't know, but whatever it was, it bleeds." He pointed to the floor, where there were bright red patches of blood, like someone had dipped a paintbrush into a can of paint and to then flick the brush at the floor.

In the wavering light of the Zippo, Jonathan spotted a body slumped on the floor near the doorway leading to the rear car and once again he handed Billy to Trudy.

Eddie spotted the body at the same time and both men worked their way to the rear of the car and leaned over the prone form.

"Oh God, it's Carlos," Jonathan said, staring down at the man's open, yet glazed-over eyes. Then he noticed the heavy dent in the man's forehead, the size and shape of the pipe Eddie held in his hand. "Eddie, look at this, this doesn't look like it was from claw marks or a fist," he said, pointing to the wound.

Eddie moved the Zippo closer and then cursed under his breath. "Shit, goddammit!" he screamed, standing up and walking away.

Jonathan stood up, too, and walked the three feet until he was back with Eddie. "What? What's wrong! You're acting pretty broken up over a guy you didn't even know," he said.

"No, you don't understand," Eddie snapped back. "I did that to him...in the dark. He must have gotten in my way. I was swinging blindly in the dark where I thought that thing was. He got in my way and I killed him. Shit!" he screamed, punching the wall.

"It's not your fault, Eddie, it's not. No one blames you," Trudy told him.

Eddie turned on her, his face wild with anger and frustration, his eyes reflecting the light of the Zippo like they were reflecting the fires of Hell. "Well, I blame me! I just killed a man in cold blood. Do you know how that makes me feel? Huh? Do you?"

Trudy shrank back and Billy let out a cry, scared. He had been doing better after Jonathan talked to him, the boy really not understanding what was really happening. Now, with Eddie screaming at him and Trudy, he began to cry again.

Jonathan grabbed Eddie's arm and spun him around. "Dammit, Eddie, get a hold of yourself. Whether you want to believe it or not, it's not your damn fault. It's that fuckin' thing that did it, whether it struck Carlos or you did. Now, pull it together, we need you. I need you...sane!"

Eddie blinked twice and he seemed to come back to himself, though there was still a light twitch to the side of his mouth. His throat moved a few times as he swallowed and then closed his eyes.

One, two, three, four, five heartbeats went by until Eddie opened his eyes and seemed more like his old self. He reached out a hand and patted Jonathan on the shoulder. "Okay, Johnny, okay. I'll get it together. You're right, there's no time for screwing around."

He looked over Jonathan's shoulder at the rear of the car, the door still open.

"Oh my God, those boys, those boys were in there. We need to see what happened to them," Eddie said and was off, running to the rear of the car, taking the only light source with him.

"Eddie, wait..." Jonathan called, but Eddie wasn't listening, the pipe leading the way as he walked through the doorway.

Jonathan shook his head. He had to give the old guy credit; he was one tough old man. He looked at Trudy, or where she should be in the now darkened car. "Trudy, you stay here, I'll be right back," he told her.

"Okay, but you be careful," she replied.

"Oh, yeah, you better believe it," he said and then moved to the rear doorway, the light of the Zippo bouncing ahead of him as Eddie walked into the next car. The others were talking together, no one wanting to move.

Upon stepping into the rear car, Jonathan moved over to Eddie. Only half the car was useable space, the other half nothing but large rocks and caved-in ceiling. In the light of the Zippo, Eddie illuminated the decapitated body of Glen.

A large pool of blood surrounded the supine body, the spilled blood now contaminated with dirt and rocks. As for Chris, he was nowhere in sight.

Jonathan leaned over the body as he stared at the jagged neck wound. "Jesus Christ, Eddie, look at this. It's like a giant razor blade just sliced his head off. What the hell is out there? What the fuck is going on here?" he asked, trying to hold it together though he was really wondering if he would just break out with the shakes and just curl up into a ball and die.

Eddie played the light over the wound. "Yeah, I see what you mean. It's like a razor just went *swipe* and took his head clean off." He frowned, shaking his head. "Poor kid, he had the rest of his life ahead of him, now it's nothing."

"What do you think happened to the other one? Chris was his name, right?" Jonathan asked.

"Don't know. Either he ran away or he was taken. Either way, he's out of our reach," Eddie said in a practical tone. It sucked but it was the truth.

Eddie stood up again, moving his hand around with the Zippo, trying to chase the shadows away. It was when he was pointing the lighter at the left side of the car that he saw an opening in the rubble.

Handing Jonathan the pipe, he moved closer. "Jonathan, look, that's how they got in. There's a hole up there. You know, we could get out that way too...if we wanted to."

"With those things out there? They'll slaughter us," Jonathan replied. "We don't even have any weapons."

Eddie turned and glared at Jonathan. "And what do you think is gonna happen if we all stay in here? Jesus, man, think of your son, for God's sake! They're picking us off one by one. We either take a chance and run for it or we're all just gonna end up dead; slaughtered like cattle waiting for the farmer to send us to the butcher!"

Anger flared in Jonathan's eyes. "I am thinking of my son, god-dammit, that's the only thing I have been thinking of since all this shit happened!" he snapped at Eddie, but then realized getting angry was a bad thing to do right now and he tried to calm down, trying to take his own advice. Only level heads would win the day. "But what about getting rescued?" Jonathan asked in a more steady tone. "Surely help is on the way by now."

"Help...help?" Eddie asked in a questioning tone. "Are you serious? Wake up, man. Even if help comes, I sure don't think it's gonna get here in time. Not by the way those things are getting the courage to come in here. By the time a rescue party arrives all they're gonna find is a few body parts and a lot of empty train cars." He lowered his voice, and tried to be more reasoning. "Look, Jonathan, I'm an old man. Even if I die tonight I've lived a good life. But you, and Trudy, your son and the others, you've all got full lives ahead of you. I don't know what's out there, but I know it's trying to kill us and has already done so on at least three occasions so far. So we need to make a decision and take it back to the others. Do we stay here and wait for the next assault? Or do we try to make a run for it?"

Jonathan bit his lip and closed his eyes, thinking, his mind filled with ideas and images. Flashes of the creature as it entered the car, all black and shiny, flew into his mind.

He remembered how it had thrown the severed head into the car as if it was playing with its food, then gulped down Glen's eyeballs like they were candy. And Eddie was right. What about Billy? He couldn't let those things get a hold of his son. He knew he'd die first before he let that happen.

Opening his eyes, he gazed back at Eddie. "All right, Eddie, I'm with you. Let's get the hell out of here."

Eddie nodded and slapped him on the left arm. "All right, that's what I'm talkin' about. Finally we're gonna do something and not just wait for it to happen. Come on, let's go back and tell the others," Eddie said happily.

Both men departed the destroyed car, closing the door as they left. They left Glen's body where they had found it. There was no material to use as a shroud and the time it would take to cover the body was better spent getting ready to leave.

Upon entering the car, all eyes looked at them, everyone glad to have some light back inside the car with them thanks to Eddie's Zippo. Power Suit Woman was curled up into a tight ball on a seat, her arms wrapped around her legs, and the two cleaners, Roselle and Caesar were leaning over Carlos' dead body.

Roselle was crying as she looked up at Jonathan. He nodded to her, trying to show his support for the loss of her friend. He hadn't known Carlos too well, but he seemed to be a good man. Trudy went over to him and Jonathan pulled her to him. Billy hugged him, too, and the three stayed that way for a brief moment, secure in each other's arms.

After a few seconds, Jonathan gently separated them from him and looked into their eyes, then turned to face the others.

"There's no sign of Chris and we already know what happened to Glen. I'm sorry, guys," he told Trudy and the others.

He remained silent as he studied the other faces around him, and then said, "Look, Eddie and I have been talking and we've decided it's for the best if we try to make a run for it. Hopefully, there's an access tunnel we can use or the cave-in isn't that bad once we get out into the tunnel. Truth is; we won't know unless we try. For all we know, there's a wide open path and all we have to do is walk through it."

"But what about staying here? Didn't you say that was the best thing to do?" Trudy asked.

Jonathan nodded. "Yeah, I did, but things have changed. What-ever's out there is coming in here to get us. We're sitting ducks in here. We've got no weapons to speak of and we're trapped with nowhere to run. The best chance for us is to try and make a run for it. Escape or die, those are our options."

Caesar and Roselle looked at Jonathan, not understanding what he was saying. He moved closer to them and pointed to each of them, then he mimicked running with his fingers, pointing outside the train. It took a second or two, but finally they understood.

"Si, Si, okay, okay," Caesar said as Roselle nodded, too. Both were smiling, trying to be strong, though Roselle still had tears on her cheeks after saying goodbye to Carlos. She was now without her jacket, and had used it to cover Carlos' body.

Jonathan smiled back and then turned to Eddie. "Okay then, now that that's decided, what's next?"

"Next we need to get some more weapons," Eddie said. "Pipes like this are good and maybe we can use some of the sheet metal in the front car as shields. After that we go."

Jonathan deferred to the older man's experience, and the two men, with Caesar now included, went into the front car to search for weapons for their desperate escape.

The first thing Eddie did upon entering the car was to find some flammable material. He wrapped the material around the end of the pipe and then lit it, an oily flame sprouting up.

"There, my lighter was getting to hot to hold," Eddie said. "We need to make some more like this, too. If those things live down here then maybe they don't like the light. I know I wouldn't."

"Good idea," Jonathan said and the three men got to work. It wasn't that hard to show Caesar what they wanted and soon the man was pulling rebar and sheet metal out of the debris, carrying it back into the main car that had become their base of operations.

Billy and Trudy stood in the doorway, watching, and Jonathan tried to send good thoughts their way, telling Billy that everything would be okay.

Twenty minutes went by, and by the time they were done, they were all hot and tired. Thirsty was another discomfort to add to the list, but there was nothing to drink.

With everyone back in the main car once again, Jonathan talked to Eddie quietly while he poked holes in sheet metal to use as handholds for the makeshift shields.

"Man, when we get out of here, I'm gonna get the biggest pitcher of beer and down it in one swallow," Jonathan said.

Eddie chuckled at that. "Yeah, I hear that. Wow, I can almost taste it now. I can't remember the last time I was this thirsty."

"I can," Jonathan said. "I was stuck on Route 93 in the middle of the summer a few years ago and there was an accident in the Sumner Tunnel. I sat there for three hours until traffic began to move. I had no water with me and my a/c was broken. After that, I always carried water in the car, just in case. Of course, something like that never happened to me again."

"Yeah, until now," Eddie said.

"Yeah, until now, thanks for pointing that out to me," Jonathan frowned.

"Happy to help," the older man quipped.

They looked at one another for a second and each man smiled, the two of them sharing a chuckle. They continued working, making weapons, with Caesar by their side, while the three women and Billy waited and watched with fear and trepidation in their eyes.

* * *

When they were finished with the weapons and shields, each man sat back and wiped their brows. Perspiration covered each of their faces, the car becoming warm as time went by.

Only the missing window on the door and a few of the smaller, broken glass squares near the ceiling let in any fresh air, and though the cool air was nice, the window was a constant threat of danger from attack.

Trudy was sitting on a seat just in front of Jonathan and they had talked a little while he worked. Eddie had listened to them, smiling now and then and sometimes had entered the conversation, giving his opinion.

The one thing that Jonathan had learned in the time he had known Eddie was that the man was very opinionated, though not so much that he became overbearing.

He had known many a man that only their opinion mattered and if you were foolish enough to ask for their opinion, well, you better take their advice or you'd never hear the end of it. Not to mention when they would just force their opinion on you whether you wanted it or not.

But Eddie was an easy going man, and once they were free of this ordeal and were safe once more, he hoped the older man would want to stay in touch with him.

Jonathan looked up at Trudy, Billy in her arms once again, and he definitely hoped she would want to stay in touch, too.

He had only known her for a short time, but the feelings were there, just like they had been with his wife when he first met her.

Trudy noticed him smiling at her and she returned it with one of her own. "What?" she asked, curious what the smile was for.

He shrugged, blushing, thankful for the dim light of the torches they had set up in the car. "I was just thinking, that's all."

"Oh, and about what may I ask?"

He swallowed hard, his pulse beating in his temple like a drum, but he forced himself to say what he was thinking. "I was just wondering if maybe, once this is all over, we could, uhm, you know, like, get a cup of coffee or something."

Her smile grew wider and she gazed down at his dirty face. "Jonathan, are you asking me out on a date?"

Scratching his head, he nodded; the butterflies in his stomach making him want to vomit. "Yeah, I guess I am."

Eddie spoke up then, true to form. "So, what do you say, honey? You gonna give the poor guy a break and say yes?"

Jonathan flashed Eddie a withering stare, but the man acted like he didn't notice it. Trudy closed her eyes, as if she was considering his proposal, and when she opened them, she gazed down on Billy's sleeping face. The boy had fallen into a restless slumber ten minutes ago, though he was constantly fidgeting in her arms.

"Well, considering I have your child in my arms, I guess I should give you a chance. Even if it's just so I can see this little guy again," she said, looking at Billy again and grinning.

"Sure, of course. That sounds great. Maybe we could go to the Museum of Science or the Aquarium or something. Billy loves those places."

Trudy nodded again. "Sure, okay, sounds fun."

"Okay then," Eddie butted in, "if you're done playing the Dating Game, what do you say we get this show on the road?"

Jonathan sighed, pulled his eyes away from Trudy's, and stood up, scrunching up his face from his frozen leg muscles. He had stayed in the same position for too long and now he had a Charlie horse.

"Okay, Eddie, let's get this done," he said as he gathered up the shields from where they lay on the floor. He was about to set the shields down onto one of the seats when one of the windows at the rear of the car exploded inward. The window was on the same side as the double doors with the already broken window.

Power Suit Woman was sitting in front of this window, her legs curled up under her as she mumbled to herself in fear, and when the window shattered, she slumped down as low as she could go, but still remained in her seat.

Though Jonathan and Caesar acted fast, running to the woman's aid as soon as the window imploded; they were still far too slow to save her.

As the window exploded inward, a large stone crashed to the floor of the car, obviously from the attacker. With lightning speed, claw-like hands reached into the car and grabbed the terrified woman by the shoulders.

She let out a squeal of anguished pain and her eyes went wide as the claws bit deep into her flesh. Then, like she was on a bungee cord that had reached its extension, she was ripped out of her seat and pulled through the window.

The last thing anyone saw was her legs, kicking erratically, one of her shoes flying off to land onto the seat she had been occupying only seconds ago.

Though she was gone, her tortured screams continued to echo in the darkness of the tunnel. But then they ceased, like someone had flicked that fateful light switch once again. One second she was screaming in pain, and then nothing, only silence.

By then Jonathan and Caesar had reached the shattered window, Eddie right behind, and all were staring out into the darkness of the tunnel. Eddie grabbed a torch, holding it just out of the window, trying to penetrate the darkness.

"Do you see her? Does anyone see her? Jesus Christ, it just took her; there was nothing we could do! It was so damn fast!" Jonathan screamed, staring out into the obsidian darkness.

Suddenly, something flew out of the darkness. It struck the train just below the broken window and fell to the tunnel floor with a meaty *thump*, before rolling away.

Eddie looked at the other two men with fear written on his features, each man gazing back with the same look. "What the hell was that?" he asked.

"Don't know. Here, give me the torch, Eddie, I want to check for myself," Jonathan said, and took the torch from the older man. Swallowing hard, with a piece of rebar in his right hand and the torch in his left, he stuck his head through the window, careful not to cut himself on the safety glass. As his head popped out of the train, he breathed in the cool, moist air, his eyes peering intently around him as he searched for movement.

Nothing moved, though he imagined monsters and demons just on the edge of where the light penetrated, just waiting to reach out and pull him from the car, to then drag him to their lair where God knew what would happen to him.

He leaned out the window and held the torch as far out as he could. Swinging it back and forth, he scanned the tunnel floor for what had struck the train.

As the torch went by the train's metal wheels, he spotted something at the edge of the light. Leaning out just a little more, he stretched his arm as far as it would go, and as he did this, the empty eye sockets of Power Suit Woman's severed head flashed back at him, the open and blood-filled sockets reflecting the light of the torch.

"Jesus Christ!" Jonathan screamed, jumping back into the car. His face was as white as a ghost's as Eddie moved next to him.

"What did you see, what did you see?" Eddie asked, almost shaking Jonathan's shoulders for an answer.

Jonathan swallowed hard, his throat dry. And when he was sure he could talk, he looked Eddie straight in the eyes. "It was her head. Jesus Christ, they cut off her fucking head, gouged out her eyes and threw it at us like it was a basketball!"

Eddie's jaw dropped. "Good God. What the hell are we dealing with out there?" he whispered.

"Did you see her? Jonathan, what happened? Is that woman all right?" Trudy asked. Billy was awake again, his eyes wide with fear. The only reason he wasn't crying was that even a small boy could get used to a situation given enough time, and as there was no apparent danger—he was sleeping when the woman was pulled through the window—he didn't feel the need to cry.

Jonathan shook his head no. "No, Trudy, she's not all right. I did see her, well, part of her anyway and I can say with an absolute certainty that she's dead."

Trudy leaned back against one of the poles lining the car for passengers to hold on to when the train was in motion.

"Oh my Lord, not her, too." She turned to look at Eddie and Jonathan. "We're all gonna die down here, aren't we." It was more of a statement than a question.

Eddie moved over to her, taking her hands in his, Billy now in the middle of them.

"Hey, now you listen to me. We're gonna get out of here. I promise. Just stay calm and be positive." Eddie turned to look at Jonathan and Caesar. "You guys ready to go? I don't think we should stay any longer than we have to. Hell, maybe they'll be busy with that woman and we can get away free and clear."

Jonathan moved next to Billy and took him back, Trudy giving him his son without protest. He hugged his son to him, almost making him cry out in pain.

"Hey, kiddo, how you doin'?" Jonathan asked Billy.

He sniffed a few times and then tried to stop crying. "I'm okay, Daddy. I'm scared though. I don't want those monsters to get me."

Jonathan rubbed his son's back, trying his best to sound strong and confident.

"And they won't. Because they have to go through me first and you know I won't let that happen. Right?"

Billy nodded slowly, then wiped his eyes with the back of his hand.

"Okay, good. Now listen. I need to give you back to Trudy so she can take care of you, okay?"

"But I want to stay with you," Billy pleaded.

"I know, sport, but I need to have my hands free in case any of those bad ol' monsters come near us. Then I'll hit them hard and make them leave us alone. How 'bout that?"

Billy thought about it for a second and then he nodded okay.

"That's a good boy," Jonathan said, handing him back to Trudy.

She took him with a smile and Jonathan gazed down at her. "I don't know what I would have done if you weren't here to help me," he said.

She shrugged. "Hey, just glad to help, now let's get out of here so you can take me on that date."

He smiled and nodded at her and then turned to face Eddie and Caesar. Eddie was looking impatient; wanting to get the show on the road.

Caesar didn't quite understand what was going on, but he saw Jonathan talking to his son and he got the idea, and so was waiting patiently for him to finish. When Jonathan nodded to him and tapped his shoulder, the man began picking up the shields and pipes.

He quickly handed one out to Eddie and Jonathan, then took one for himself.

Trudy didn't carry anything as she had her hands full holding Billy.

"You know, we never even knew that woman's name," Jonathan said to Eddie.

"Huh, really? Wow, you're right, we didn't. Shit, to die without a name, that's terrible." He grabbed a torch and handed one to Jonathan and one to Roselle, then the small group moved to the newly shattered window. "At least they made it easier for us to get out of the train," Eddie said almost cheerfully. The torch in his hands sputtered and sparked.

There wasn't much to burn so they had taken Roselle's jacket off of Carlos as well as the dead man's shirt. Then each of the surviving passengers had donated something from their own clothing. Jonathan and Eddie had lost their socks, and Trudy had given up the sweater she had worn under her jacket.

Caesar had donated his shirt; his jacket wasn't the same brand as Carlos' and Roselle's was, and if it wasn't flammable, it was useless for the cause.

Eddie stuck the torch out the broken window and peered into the darkness. He counted to ten before sticking his head back into the car. "Looks clear," he said, "I'll go out first and then you guys can follow me."

"Okay, but be careful," Jonathan told the old man. Eddie nodded and slipped a leg through the window, then dropped the torch onto the tunnel floor. He waited again for signs of movement, but when nothing stirred, he swung the other leg over the sill and dropped to the tunnel floor with a soft crunching of rocks under his feet.

Crouching in the light of the torch, he swallowed hard, anticipating being discovered at any second, but saying a silent thanks when he wasn't. "Okay, come on down, the coast is clear," he whispered up to the others.

Caesar was next, followed by Roselle. They each slid out of the window effortlessly. Billy was dropped down to the tunnel floor next, Roselle taking him for a moment.

Jonathan followed and he handed his torch out the window to Caesar and then slid out one leg at a time, careful of the glass. Once he was out, he waved up to Trudy who was standing in the window, her face a mask of apprehension.

"Come on, hurry up. So far so good," Jonathan called to her.

She nodded and quickly did as the rest had done, with the exception her skirt caught on a piece of the safety glass still in the window frame and it was ripped. Ignoring it, she dropped to the tunnel floor, Jonathan there to catch her. Once down, she took Billy from Roselle, thanking the woman for her help.

When the group was all together once more, they began to move off to the rear of the train.

Eddie's torch began to flicker, and then it went out, the material totally consumed by the fire. He pulled out one last sock from a pocket and wrapped it around the end of the pipe. He pulled his Zippo out of his pocket and tried to light the torch again. The Zippo sparked a few times but didn't light. "Shit, the damn things out of fluid," he said in the dark.

Jonathan moved next to him and held his torch under Eddie's.

"Here, let me light it, we should be fine as long as at least one torch is always lit."

Once Eddie's torch was lit again, they began moving down the tunnel. They had only reached the end of the second car behind the one they had used as their base when it was apparent they wouldn't be going any further.

The entire car was buried under rubble, large boulders, piping and wiring from the overhead ceiling of the tunnel covering everything on both sides of the train.

"Dammit. Well, we knew it might be blocked. Let's try the front of the train. Maybe it's better up there," Eddie said, taking the lead.

The five survivors, and Billy, trudged back the way they had come, passing the car they'd holed up in, and then continued onward to the front of the train.

Just as they passed the second car, Jonathan raised his hand for them to stop. "Wait, I see something in the wall over there," he said, pointing ten feet away to the right.

"What did you see? Was it them?" Eddie hissed.

Jonathan shook his head. "No, it's something else, come on, I want to check it out. Maybe it's a way out."

They followed Jonathan away from the train until he was standing at the tunnel wall. Where the wall had once been smooth, with no openings, now there was a large crack in its facade, the crack no more than a foot wide.

There were large splatters of blood covering the edges of the wide crack, like something human had been forced in there without its consent and the flesh had been caught on the sharp edges of the stones.

Jonathan leaned closer and then pulled his nose back, the charnel house smell coming from the crack overwhelming. As the others noticed the odor of decay, everyone began gagging, trying not to throw up.

"Oh my Lord, what is that awful smell?" Trudy asked, covering her nose. Billy buried his face into her jacket, trying to stop the smell from penetrating his sinus cavity.

Eddie was the one who answered. "I know what that smell is. That's the smell of death. I've smelled that odor before in the war. It's when corpses and pieces of corpses would lie out in the sun for days on end, that's what that smell's like."

Jonathan was already backing up, deciding this wasn't a way out, when he spotted something on the ground, reflecting the torchlight.

Leaning over, his eyes went wide when he saw it was a pistol, the holster it had been in lying next to it. On the holster was the picture of a steer and he knew who the weapon belonged to.

The Transit cop.

Jonathan quickly reasoned out what must have happened. When the cop had been taken from the train, he must have been dragged this way and had lost his weapon. Evidently, the creatures didn't know what they had left behind. Picking up the gun, he showed it to the others.

"Well, well, look at what I found?"

Eddie moved up next to him and whistled softly. "Outstanding, great job. But let me ask you something. Do you know how to use that?"

Jonathan realized that, no, he didn't. He had fired a few hand-guns at the gun range a few times with friend's years ago, but he was far from proficient with firearms.

In fact, the handgun he had at the house had never been fired. When he was going to kill himself with it a year ago, that would have been its first time being used.

Eddie saw the look on Jonathan's face and he nodded, clicking his teeth. "Uh-huh, that's what I thought. Why don't you let me handle that and you take the torch so I can see."

Jonathan reluctantly gave the pistol to Eddie, who upon taking it, quickly popped out the clip and checked the chamber, then slapped the clip back in, cocked the weapon, and then gazed back at Jonathan.

At that moment Jonathan saw the young man Eddie had once been. The man who had gone to war and had seen things Jonathan could only imagine.

"This is a Glock 9mm," Eddie said. "It has seventeen rounds in the clip and has good stopping power. When you get hit by this, you don't usually get up and dance the jig, if you know what I mean. It should do the job nicely." He grinned widely, his teeth reflecting the torchlight. "I'll tell you one thing, I sure as hell feel a lot better. Just let those bastards try something now."

As if something in the dark was answering his challenge, running footsteps could be heard moving across the gravel.

Caesar yelled something in Spanish, and a second later, everyone was looking around in fear, trying to peer past the glare of the torches.

"Oh my God, it's them! Jonathan, what do we do?" Trudy asked in a panic.

Roselle and Caesar stood next to her, holding one another, though Caesar had his right hand held in front of him, the torch waving back and forth, the left holding a shield.

He moved away from Roselle and pulled the piece of rusted rebar from the belt of his pants. Waving the rebar in front of him menacingly, he called out to the darkness in Spanish.

Though Jonathan didn't know what the man was saying, he had a pretty good idea. He was saying, "Come on you bastards, I'm ready for you!"

Eddie waved the gun around, searching for a target, but all he found were shifting shadows that seemed to appear at the edge of the light and then dart backwards to vanish again. They were so fast he wondered if he was imagining them.

"Dammit, I can't see shit, they're so damn fast! They could be anywhere!" Eddie yelled. "Everyone, get over here by me and let's get to the front of the train. Maybe we can find an opening in the cave-in up there."

Jonathan patted Caesar's shoulder, pointing to Eddie and motioning with his hand that they were going to go over to the front of the train.

The man nodded, and ever so slowly, the group began moving again with Eddie trying to cover all vulnerable positions at the same time.

The noises surrounding them began to grow. A tapping began, as if long nails were impatiently rapping on a piece of sheet metal. But there had to be at least half a dozen hands doing the tapping, and in less than a minute, the entire tunnel was filled with the noise.

Like smaller scale African drums, the tapping continued and Eddie lost a small piece of his nerve and shot the gun into the darkness. One, two, three, four times he fired, the gunshots echoing like a cannon had gone off. If he hit anything, there was no sign.

Trudy moved next to Jonathan, Billy cowering in her arms. "Oh my God, Jonathan, what's going on? Maybe we should get back inside the train."

"No!" Eddie snapped. "That would be a mistake. We're in this for the long haul, people. It's now or never, now stop talking and get moving. Jonathan, stay with Caesar and cover our backs. And give Roselle one of the torches so I can see up here."

Jonathan did as ordered, the tone of Eddie's voice making him do it without thinking. Eddie was in battle mode now, like he was back in the war against the Germans.

Only this time the enemy was an unknown force, and if they were taken prisoner, there would be no mercy, only a terrible, suffering death.

Roselle moved up next to Eddie as they all slid their feet across the gravel of the tunnel floor. Shadows danced just out of sight of the perimeter of the torches and Eddie fired off another two shots, though once again, nothing was hit.

"Dammit, where are they?" he asked, sweat beading on his forehead.

Roselle moved to his side, and without realizing it, she began moving out and away from the rest of the group. She became like a baby goat in a herd, the wolf spotting the lone animal wandering away from the pack, the perfect target.

Eddie noticed she was almost five feet away from him and he was just about to call out to her, wanting to tell her to get back next to him, when a flash of something obsidian charged into Roselle, knocking the torch from her hand.

She let out a screech of surprise and then she was gone, carried off into the darkness.

"Roselle!" Eddie screamed and began firing in the direction he thought she had been taken, each gunshot lighting up the tunnel like a flash of lightning.

"No, stop, Eddie, you'll hit her, too!" Jonathan yelled out.

Eddie stopped firing and turned to Jonathan. "Well, what the hell am I supposed to do? Wave goodbye to her and leave it at that!"

"No, of course not, but what if you shoot her in the dark?"

"Jonathan, if we can't get her back, she's dead anyway," he snapped back, the fear clear on his face in the flickering torchlight.

From somewhere in the darkness, there was a high-pitched scream and Caesar called out to Roselle. There was no return answer.

Seconds passed and each of them stood perfectly still. The torchlight was like a small island in the ocean of darkness with sharks all around them, prepared to pounce at any second.

The tension was maddening, and finally, after three minutes of nothing happening, a round object flew out of the darkness to land on the tunnel floor in front of the group. It rolled a few feet until it stopped in front of Jonathan.

Moving the torch closer to the object, he had a feeling he knew what it was before the actual image was fully inside his mind.

It was Roselle's head, her long hair draped messily over her face. Her mouth was open, turned up in a last scream, frozen forever in time, but it was her eye sockets, the eyes missing once more, that was the most chilling sight to behold.

She had been decapitated, de-eyed, and then the head had been tossed back to the others like a toy, used to taunt and terrorize.

Whatever these creatures were, they were now playing with Jonathan and the others. Caesar gazed down at the severed head of Roselle and he fell to his knees, his hands hovering over the head, as if he was afraid to touch it.

Tears fell down his cheeks and he pulled a gold cross from under his shirt, kissing it softly. When he stood back up, his face went from one of sorrow to one of anger.

He glared at Jonathan in the gloom, his face a mask of loss, and handed his torch to Jonathan, who took it, not understanding what the other man wanted to do.

Caesar raised the piece of rebar he was holding over his head with both hands, and with a snarl of sorrow and frustration, he charged out of the circle of torchlight, and into the tunnel before any of the others could even think of stopping him.

He was screaming long and loud at the top of his lungs, the Spanish unintelligible, but the tone of his voice clear to his meaning.

"For Roselle!" he yelled, wanting vengeance for his fallen friend, swinging the metal rebar like a warrior going into battle, and at that moment, Jonathan wondered if perhaps the two cleaners had been lovers.

Thirty seconds went by, Caesar's voice echoing off the tunnel walls and the sound of the rebar clanking on rocks and sometimes something fleshier, meatier. Then it stopped, like that ill-fated light switch had been flicked yet again.

There were sounds of scrabbling and scuffling in the darkness, the entire group remaining motionless, too scared to move.

"Caesar! You all right?" Jonathan called out, not really expecting an answer.

Trudy moved next to him, trying to get into his arms, but with the two torches and the piece of rebar in his hands, Jonathan couldn't hold her.

He looked down at Billy and his heart broke.

How was he going to get his son out of this impossible situation?

There was the sound of a meaty *thwack*, and a second later, another object flew out of the darkness. This time the object was thrown too hard and Jonathan had to be the one to dodge out of the way or risk being struck.

The object just missed his head and bounced off the wall of the tunnel. When it came to rest on the floor, he held the torch over it. It was Caesar's severed, bloody head, minus the eyes, and the tongue was hanging out at an odd angle.

"Oh my God, oh no!" Trudy cried out and tried to get behind Jonathan.

"You bastards!" Eddie screamed into the blackness. "You bastards!" he repeated and then fired three more shots into the dark. With the exception of the ricocheting bullets echoing through the tunnel, there was no outcry that he had hit anything.

Silently, a large rock flew past Eddie's head and he ducked instinctually. Another, smaller rock flew out of the darkness and struck Jonathan on the shoulder. He cried out and tried to shrink away, but there was nowhere to go so he just made sure Billy and Trudy were behind him, safe from the onslaught.

In the circle of light, they were like fish in a barrel to their hunters. They were helpless.

"Come on, we have to make a run for the front of the train!" Eddie yelled out, firing two quick shots over his shoulder.

The three remaining adults ran for it, the torches in Jonathan's hands flickering from the wind of his running, threatening to go out and plunge them all into perpetual darkness.

In Trudy's arms, Billy screamed in fear, his voice filled with the terror they were all feeling. Jonathan wanted to console his son, but there was no time. Now they needed to run.

More rocks landed around them as they tried to escape, and Trudy cried out when one struck her right leg, blood seeping from the wound. But there was no time to check how bad it was. All they could do was run and hope for the best.

Eddie fired one more round over their heads, hoping to keep the creatures at bay, and then they were at the front of the train, and once again there was nothing but rubble blocking the tunnel on both sides.

To their left, the train was a flattened mess of metal and steel, and if there was an opening somewhere, it would take hours of excavating to try and find it.

"Dammit, no!" Eddie screamed, slapping the rubble with his hand. "There's no way out. The entire tunnel has collapsed in on itself. Good God, how the hell did this happen?"

Scratching and scraping from behind made them turn around, their backs to the rubble as they gazed out into the darkness. Jonathan handed Eddie one of the torches and the older man took it, waving it back and forth in his left hand, the gun in his right and aimed into the abyss.

Jonathan made Trudy and Billy hide behind him, as if his body alone could shield them from danger.

Then they waited, one second at a time. A few sounds could be heard in the darkness and Eddie fired a round or two in the estimated direction.

One time he was greeted with a high-pitched scream and he laughed out loud. "Ha, there ya go, ya bastards! How do you like it! Try to get us and you'll get some more of that!" He fired again at the shadows in his enthusiasm, but hit nothing for his trouble.

But after that one incident, there was only silence. Whether it was because they now respected the three survivors with the weapon that shot liquid fire or not, was unknown, but for whatever reason, there were no more rocks thrown and nothing tried to attack them.

The three frightened adults and one child waited with their backs to the rubble, shivering in fear and the dampness of the tunnel. In the train they had been relatively warm, but inside the tunnel it was moist and cool and the darkness only made it seem worse.

"What are they waiting for, Jonathan?" Trudy whispered, sniffing from crying. "Why don't they just get it over with?"

Billy was curled up in Jonathan's arms. The small boy had passed out from exhaustion a few minutes ago, not able to keep up the state of alertness required by the others.

"I don't know," Eddie said. "Maybe they're scared of us." He waved the gun back and forth. His arm was killing him and he didn't know how much longer he could keep it up. It was almost a half hour since they reached the front of the tunnel and he was all out of ideas as to what they could do to escape.

Jonathan stared at his torch, watching the small flame dance in the darkness. It was going to go out soon, so he carefully took off his coat, took out anything in his pockets that mattered, and wrapped it around the end of the torch, careful not to extinguish the flame by accident.

A second later and the torch was burning brightly again, casting a wider circle of illumination out in front of them. As the circle of light grew larger, all three adults gasped when they saw they were completely surrounded by the creatures.

Just before the torchlight pushed the creatures backwards, Jonathan got a quick glimpse of the beings that were hunting him.

He saw that creatures were the same size as him and Eddie, but some were larger and some smaller. Their skin appeared to be covered with oil or some other dark viscous fluid, giving them their obsidian look. They had heads the same size as he did and their arms and legs were proportioned to an average human being.

Though hard to believe it, what he saw was essentially a human being, or what had once been one at some time in the past. But now this tribe of tunnel dwellers was nothing more than beasts hunting for food.

How they had arrived here and why no one had ever seen them before was a mystery, but not one he cared to contemplate at the moment.

For now, all he wanted to do was get past them.

"Jesus Christ, did you see their eyes?" Eddie whispered as he waved the gun before him.

Jonathan nodded. Yes he had, but there had been too much to take in at once. Their eyes had been very odd. They had been all white, and had almost glowed when the torchlight touched them.

He could only assume it was from living in perpetual darkness their entire lives, never seeing the sun or perhaps light of any kind.

At least, until now.

"Jonathan, my torch is dying, I need something to keep it going," Eddie said worriedly.

"Here, take this," Trudy whispered, sliding out of her coat. Billy stirred in her arms, but thankfully remained asleep.

Thank heaven for small blessings, Jonathan thought. At least his son was oblivious to what was happening.

Taking the coat from Trudy, Eddie inspected the material to make sure it would burn. It was some kind of cotton blend and should burn well when added to the torch.

He wrapped it around the torch slowly, and a second later it flared higher, pushing the darkness back another four feet.

At the ring of the circle of light, the creatures reared up and hissed, this time flashing their sharpened teeth, each one filed to wicked points. In the light and shadows, Jonathan thought they looked like vampires, though of course that was entirely ridiculous.

One of the creatures tried to swipe at the torch Eddie was holding and the old man shot it in the face. The creature flew backwards into its brethren and a loud hiss filled the tunnel as the others glared at the offending humans.

"I don't think they liked that," Jonathan told Eddie, his voice a fraction away from cracking into madness.

"Ya think?" Eddie snapped back.

Without warning, lightning fast, a blur came out of the darkness on Eddie's left side, the movement so quick that even in full daylight the motion would have been difficult to see.

Eddie's out-stretched gun arm wavered in the torchlight for another second, before it was sliced off just above the elbow, the severed limb falling to the tunnel floor.

Eddie screamed in mortal pain, blood shooting out of the stump like a geyser. Turning to Jonathan, he dropped the torch in his other hand and sprayed the younger man's face with blood like he was holding a fire hose, and Jonathan felt the warm sticky blood fill his mouth and nose.

Sputtering the blood out of his mouth, Jonathan tried to figure out what just happened to his friend. Eddie's face was absolute insanity incarnate, his eyes so wide his eyes balls were ready to just pop out of his head.

There was a large vein on the side of his forehead that was thumping steadily in rhythm to his pulse. Jonathan saw the stump where the man's arm used to be and he screamed as well, totally losing it for a moment in the terror of the situation.

Trudy screamed behind him. Not quite understanding what was happening, but knowing it was bad.

Eddie was lost in a world of pain without reason. He took one look at Jonathan, his eyes not actually seeing him, and he ran off and out of the torchlight.

He didn't make it more than five steps before he was pounced on by the creatures like a lion would a wounded zebra.

In the edges of the flickering torchlight, Jonathan stared in utter horror as Eddie was ripped into and gutted like a fish. His head was pulled from his shoulders after a neat slice across the jugular.

Blood shot outward for a second, and then one of the creatures leaned over and began to drink, slopping up the scarlet fluid like it was rare wine.

Jonathan's voice was gone as he stood utterly helpless. If the creatures had wanted him, Billy and Trudy at that moment, they could have easily taken them.

But they didn't. It seemed that at the present time, they were pleased to play with Eddie, feeding on his desecrated corpse.

Jonathan watched as one of the creatures picked up Eddie's head, and with one long nail that was trimmed like a dagger, plucked out each of the old man's eyes.

With a low moan of pleasure, and just like they were candy, it popped the orbs into its mouth, leaning back its head as it enjoyed the delicacy. Bits of white goop slid out of the corner of its lips to drip onto the tunnel floor.

When it was finished eating, it chucked the head away like a discarded shell, finished with its meal.

"Oh my God," Jonathan said as he stared at the creature. "Oh my God."

He fell to his butt, his back leaning against the rubble, and Trudy crawled next to him for comfort, Billy thankfully still asleep.

The torch Eddie had been holding sputtered on the ground, and then slowly, it died. Now only the torch in Jonathan's shaking hand seemed to be keeping the creatures at bay, and after the way they had attacked Eddie, he wasn't too confident that the light was really working that well as a deterrent.

Trudy nuzzled her face next to Jonathan's cheek and he wrapped his arm around her. In the circle of light, he began counting the creatures as they swayed back and forth at the perimeter of the torch's glow He stopped counting at twelve. After that, what would be the point? Whether there was five or five hundred, there was no way he could stop them all.

Even if he had a fully loaded gun there were just too damn many to fight.

Wait, the gun!

His eyes went to the ground, searching for it, and there it was, still in Eddie's hand, the severed arm lying on the tunnel floor. Swallowing hard, he reached out the three feet separating him from the gun, expecting to see a blur in the darkness and then his own arm would become separated from his body.

But for whatever reason, he reached the arm and gently slid it across the gravel unmolested. When he had it in his grip, he pried the gun from Eddie's hand, the fingers locked around the trigger in a death grip.

Tears appeared on Jonathan's face and he tried to fight them off. He needed to focus on what he was doing. Prying one finger at a time, he finally managed to get the gun out of the dead hand and he tossed the arm at the creatures angrily.

They jumped out of the way, but once they realized what it was, they jumped on it, devouring it like it was a turkey leg at Thanksgiving dinner.

He felt only slightly more secure with the gun in his hand, as it was almost useless against such odds.

"What are they waiting for?" Trudy sniffed, hugging Billy tightly. "Why don't they just finish it?"

"I don't know, honey, I truly don't know," he whispered, his voice cracking. "We just have to wait."

* * *

They sat for thirty more minutes and no attack came, and despite himself, he began to feel sleepy. No one could maintain the constant state of alertness he needed to keep up; it was physically impossible. Next to him, Billy was awake and crying again. He took his son from Trudy and handed her the torch.

"Daddy, why are we still here? What happened to Eddie? Did those monsters eat him? I don't want to be eaten, Daddy, I just don't," he cried.

Tears welled up within Jonathan's eyes as he gazed at his son's dirty face in the flickering shadows of the remaining torch.

It was almost ready to go out.

Everything worthy of burning had been burned in the past half hour, all three of them now clothed in nothing but their underwear. And he knew what would happen when that torch finally went out.

Trying to hold back the sobs filling his chest, he shook his head back and forth.

"And you won't be, Billy. Didn't I say that wouldn't happen to you? Huh, didn't I?"

Billy nodded, his nose running and his eyes red from crying almost non-stop.

"Now listen to me, son. I need you to be brave for me, okay? I promise I'll see you safe, I promise."

Trudy was crying next to him and he wrapped his arm around her, placing the Glock on the ground. It was useless anyway, there were far too many of them to stop. Plus, Eddie had fired so many times he had no way of even knowing how many bullets were left; couldn't be that many, anyway.

Trudy looked up and into his eyes, the shadows deepening as the torch began to flicker and fade. "I don't think we're gonna be going on that date after all, huh," she said to him in a shaky voice.

He hugged her closer. "No, I don't think we are. Tell you what," he grinned slightly. "What do you say we call this our first date and leave it at that?"

She nodded, the motion making her face rub against his cheek. He turned to face her, and their lips were no more than an inch apart.

Right now, at this moment, all his inhibitions were gone. There was nothing to save them for.

"I could have loved you, you know," he whispered. "I didn't think there would ever be anyone after my wife died, but now, I know I could have loved you."

He cried some more, the tears falling onto his shoulder and she nodded, as well.

"I could have loved you, too. Both of you," she said, nuzzling Billy's hair.

The torchlight began to flicker some more, and as it did, the creatures moved a step closer, slowly surrounding them until they were only a few feet away.

They were all crying now that they knew what was to come and Jonathan's hand reached out for the Glock on the tunnel floor. Picking it up, he brought it close to Trudy's eyes so she could see it.

She stared at the gun for a full five seconds.

And then she nodded.

Jonathan took Billy off his lap and he set him on the ground next to him.

"Billy, would you do me a favor?" he asked in a sweet voice, though he was shaking so hard he could barely maintain the tone, tears filling his eyes like they would never end.

"Sure, Daddy, okay. Hey, Daddy, what are those monsters doing over there? You go away monsters. You leave me and my Daddy alone!" Billy yelled at the creatures. He looked up at Jonathan. "There, Daddy, I'll make sure they don't hurt us," he said, his voice high and sweet with youth and wonder. "Don't cry Daddy, it'll be all right, I'll protect you, too."

"Thank you, Billy, that was great," Jonathan smiled, the tears pouring out of his eyes. "Now do me that favor. Turn around and close your eyes for me and think of Mommy, okay. Would you like that? Would you like to see Mommy again?"

He nodded, the back of his head moving up and down. "Yes, Daddy, I would. Can we go see Mommy now?"

Jonathan slowly raised the Glock to the back of his son's head and then had to use the other hand, as well; his right arm and hand were shaking so hard.

"Yes, honey, just close your eyes and think of Mommy and you'll be with her soon." He let out a slight sob that wanted to be a roar of anguish, and he squeezed the trigger on the handgun as he screamed at the ceiling of the tunnel.

He had to look away, not able to see the results of the bullet penetrating his son's head, and still without looking, he turned to Trudy. She caressed his cheek with her hand, tears flooding down her face in rivers, and she kissed him once more, softly and tenderly.

It was a kiss that would last a lifetime...and an eternity.

"See you soon?" she asked, her shoulders shaking as she cried.

He nodded, crying so hard he could barely see straight, and the tears filled his eyes to the point that everything was just a blur. "You bet, see you soon," he said in a whisper.

She turned around so the back of her head was facing him, and in the shadows of the dying torch, her shoulders shook as she sobbed softly.

She crossed herself and mumbled an Amen and then she whispered to him. "Whenever you're ready," she said, but the second she had uttered the word *ready*, he squeezed the trigger. Her head shot forward and she fell to the tunnel floor, her fingers spasming as her nerves shut down.

He screamed once more, long and loud, his heart actually breaking in half inside his chest.

He reached out for Billy's limp body and pulled him to his lap, cradling his son's dead body in his arms, rocking him back and forth as blood seeped from the jagged hole in his son's head and soaked into his underwear and coated his legs.

"There, son, now you're with Mommy," he said in gasps of strangled breaths, crying so hard he couldn't breathe.

The torch flickered briefly and finally, with one last sputter, it died, and he heard the sounds of clawed feet scratching on the rocks in front of him.

They were coming for him.

Though he thought he could do it, just close his eyes and let them take him in the darkness, he realized he still couldn't let go of his life in the inky blackness and he remembered the cell phone he had found in the front car of the train earlier; the phone now sitting under his left butt cheek.

When he had burned his jacket, he had slid the phone into his pants pocket and had then placed it on the ground when his pants had needed to be burned, as well.

Picking up the phone, he flipped it open, the small screen lighting up and pushing the darkness away, but only slightly. The creatures stopped and stared at him, this man who was lying there on the tunnel floor crying, now seeming to be unafraid of them.

Jonathan waved the cell phone in his left hand, moving it back and forth across the visages of the creatures that were only inches from his face.

They swayed back and forth, staring at him and at the phone, fascinated, their eyes wide, their white orbs watching him like he was an ant under a microscope.

With his right hand, he raised the Glock to his lips and placed it inside his mouth. The barrel burned his mouth, the weapon still hot from the recent firings, and he squeezed his eyes shut. The tears had stopped now; he was all out of them.

He held the gun in his mouth for how long, he had no idea, but just when the cell phone began to beep, **Low Battery**, and prepared to die, he did the same, his finger beginning to tighten on the trigger of the gun.

With one final sob, he squeezed the trigger on the Glock.

But instead of a loud noise in his ears as a bullet blasted his brains out the back of his skull, and the sweet oblivion of death took him into its cold embrace, he heard a dry click. The gun was empty, he was out of bullets.

He began to laugh, long and hard, and while he cradled his son in his arms, he yelled out his frustration. "Come on then, kill me! That's what you want to do, right? Well then fucking do it!"

None of the creatures moved; but merely stood watching him, swaying back and forth like cornstalks on a windy day. The cell phone was ready to turn off for good, and then the rubble behind him began to shift. Stones were pulled inward as slowly but surely, a hole was beginning to form. The creatures hissed and backed away from him, though only a few feet more. Still, they had retreated.

As the rubble shifted behind him, he slid a foot away from the tumbling debris, his son still cradled in his arms.

If the rubble was moving, then it could only mean one thing.

His jaw dropped and his face went ash white. No, it couldn't be. Not now! Not when his son was gone! Not after he'd killed him!

"No, oh God, no. Not now. Not when it's too late!" Jonathan screamed to the forming hole. He turned to the creatures, his eyes filled with anger and loss.

"Not now, not when it doesn't matter. Why didn't you just kill me when you had the chance! Why did you wait?" he screamed at them. The creatures hissed and swayed, watching the rubble disappear as a small hole began to appear in the side of the cave-in.

Though filled with sadness and loss, the will to survive was strong in him, and though he didn't know how he would go on living after everything that had happened, he moved to the hole, something inside him still happy to be alive and finally rescued.

Ever so gently, he put Billy down on the ground, careful not to jar him, like his son was just sleeping. The cell phone beeped again, warning of its impending death, and he aimed it at the opening in the rubble.

"Oh thank God, I'm here, I'm in here! Help me!" he called out, now wanting to live more than ever, no matter what. He realized it was easy to be brave and face death when there was nothing to live for, but still, he wanted to live! He didn't want to die!

He looked down at the still forms of Trudy and his son, and though it broke his heart to leave them, he wanted to live even more.

The opening was now large enough for him to fit through, the workers still moving rocks and debris from the other side, and he stuck his head and shoulders through the opening, the cell phone now in front of him so he could see. He tried not to think about the creatures behind him and how they could grab his feet at any time if they wanted to.

The phone beeped again, warning him that it was really going to stop working soon, and just before it died, the screen showed him his rescuers at the opposite end of the hole as they moved the last of the rubble blocking his path to freedom.

The dim screen of the cell phone illuminated the opening and his rescuers clearly in its pale ambience. Just as the battery died, turning the phone off forever, Jonathan screamed as the black claws and milk-white eyes came for him, grabbing him by the head and shoulders, and pulling him deeper into the darkness he'd longed for only seconds before.

THE WAR AGAINST THEM: A ZOMBIE NOVEL
by Jose Alfredo Vazquez

Mankind wasn't prepared for the onslaught.

An ancient organism is reanimating the dead bodies of its victims, creating worldwide chaos and panic as the disease spreads to every corner of the globe. As governments struggle to contain the disease, courageous individuals across the planet learn what it truly means to make choices as they struggle to survive.

Geopolitics meet technology in a race to save mankind from the worst threat it has ever faced. Doctors, military and soldiers from all walks of life battle to find a cure. For the dead walk, and if not stopped, they will wipe out all life on Earth. Humanity is fighting a war they cannot win, for who can overcome Death itself? Man versus the walking dead with the winner ruling the planet. Welcome to *The War Against Them*.

THE TURNING: A STORY OF THE LIVING DEAD
by Kelly M. Hudson

The Dead Walk!

And no place on earth is safe from their ravening hunger. Civilization falls, leaving groups of struggling survivors to navigate a world that has descended into Hell.

Jeff Richards is one such survivor. He and his lover Jenny flee their home in the Bay Area and take a perilous journey through Northern California into Oregon, seeking shelter in rural areas to avoid both the living dead and that most treacherous animal of all: their fellow humans.

But can a man who has lost everything, including his humanity, ever be reborn?

When the dead walk, will any of us survive?

Or will we all join the ranks of the undead to forever walk the earth.

END OF DAYS: AN APOCALYPTIC ANTHOLOGY
VOLUMES 1-3

Edited by Anthony Giangregorio

Our world is a fragile place.

Meteors, famine, floods, nuclear war, solar flares, and hundreds of other calamities can plunge our small blue planet into turmoil in an instant.

What would you do if tomorrow the sun went super nova or the world was swallowed by water, submerging the world into the cold darkness of the ocean? This anthology explores some of those scenarios and plunges you into total annihilation.

But remember, it's only a book, and tomorrow will come as it always does.

Or will it?

KINGDOM OF THE DEAD
by Anthony Giangregorio
THE DEAD HAVE RISEN!

In the dead city of Pittsburgh, two small enclaves struggle to survive, eking out an existence of hand to mouth.

But instead of working together, both groups battle for the last remaining fuel and supplies of a city filled with the living dead.

Six months after the initial outbreak, a lone helicopter arrives bearing two more survivors and a newborn baby. One enclave welcomes them, while the other schemes to steal their helicopter and escape the decaying city.

With no police, fire, or social services existing, the two will battle for dominance in the steel city of the walking dead. But when the dust settles, the question is: will the remaining humans be the winners, or the losers?

When the dead walk, the line between Heaven and Hell is so twisted and bent there is no line at all.

RISE OF THE DEAD
by Anthony Giangregorio
DEATH IS ONLY THE BEGINNING!

In less than forty-eight hours, more than half the globe was infected.

In another forty-eight, the rest would be enveloped.

The reason?

A science experiment gone horribly wrong which enabled the dead to walk, their flesh rotting on their bones even as they seek human prey.

Jeremy was an ordinary nineteen year old slacker. He partied too much and had done poorly in high school. After a night of drinking and drugs, he awoke to find the world a very different place from the one he'd left the night before.

The dead were walking and feeding on the living, and as Jeremy stepped out into a world gone mad, the dead spotting him alone and unarmed in the middle of the street, he had to wonder if he would live long enough to see his twentieth birthday.

THE CHRONICLES OF JACK PRIMUS
BOOK ONE
by Michael D. Griffiths

Beneath the world of normalcy we all live in lies another world, one where supernatural beings exist. These creatures of the night hunt us; want to feed on our very souls, though only a few know of their existence.

One such man is Jack Primus, who accidentally pierces the veil between this world and the next. With no other choice if he wants to live, he finds himself on the run, hunted by beings called the Xemmoni, an ancient race that sees humans as nothing but cattle. They want his soul, to feed on his very essence, and they will kill all who stand in their way. But if they thought Jack would just lie down and accept his fate, they were sorely mistaken. He didn't ask for this battle, but he knew he would fight them with everything at his disposal, for to lose is a fate worse than death.

He would win this war, and he would take down anyone who got in his way.

ETERNAL NIGHT: A VAMPIRE ANTHOLOGY

Edited by Anthony Giangregorio

Blood, fangs, darkness and terror...these are the calling cards of the vampire mythos.

Inside this tome are stories that embrace vampire history but seek to introduce a new literary spin on this longstanding fictional monster. Follow a dark journey through cigarette-smoking creatures hunted by rogue angels, vampires that feed off of thoughts instead of blood, immortals presenting the fantastic in a local rock band, to a legendary monster on the far reaches of town.

Forget what you know about vampires; this anthology will destroy historical mythos and embrace incredible new twists on this celebrated, fictional character.

Welcome to a world of the undead, welcome to the world of *Eternal Night*.

DEAD HISTORY 2

A Zombie Anthology

Edited by Anthony Giangregorio

From the dawn of mankind, the walking dead have been with us.

The greatest moments in history are not what they appear.

Through the ages, the undead have been there, only the proof has been erased, documents destroyed, and witnesses silenced.

The living dead is man's greatest secret.

In this tome, are a few of the stories of what really happened all those years ago. History isn't alive, it's dead!

INSIDE THE PERIMETER: SCAVENGERS OF THE DEAD

by Alan Spencer

In the middle of nowhere, the vestiges of an abandoned town are surrounded by inescapably high concrete barriers, permitting no trespass or escape. The town is dormant of human life, but rampant with the living dead, who choose not to eat flesh, but to instead continue their survival by cruder means.

Boyd Broman, a detective arrested and falsely imprisoned, has been transferred into the secret town. He is given an ultimatum: recapture Hayden Grubaugh, the cannibal serial killer, who has been banished to the town, in exchange for his freedom.

During Boyd's search, he discovers why the psychotic cannibal must really be captured and the sinister secrets the dead town holds.

With no chance of escape, Broman finds himself trapped among the ravenous, violent dead. With the cannibal feeding on the animated cadavers and the undead searching for Boyd, he must fulfill his end of the deal before the rotting corpses turn him into an unwilling organ donor.

But Boyd wasn't told that no one gets out alive, that the town is a death sentence. For there is no escape from *Inside the Perimeter*.

PLAYING GOD: A ZOMBIE NOVEL
by Jeffery Dye

It was supposed to be a regeneration virus to help soldiers on the battlefield—regrowing limbs and healing wounds— but a simple act of carelessness unleashed it on an unsuspecting world.

For the virus was not perfected, and once exposed, the host quickly dies, only to rise again as one of the undead.

As countries are quickly overrun, scientists and military teams battle to contain the outbreak.

There is no other option.

If the infection continues to spread, soon the entire globe will be consumed. And perhaps that will be a just punishment for a mankind that dared to try to play God.

DEAD HOUSE: A ZOMBIE GHOST STORY
by Keith Adam Luethke

The old mansion on the edge of town, aptly named Dead House, has a history of blood, pain, and death, but what Victor Leeds knows of this past only scratches the surface of the true horrors within.

But when his girlfriend is attacked by a shadowy figure one rainy night, he soon finds himself caught up in a world where the dead walk and ghostly wraiths abound. And to make matters worse, a pair of serial killers are fulfilling carefully made plans, and when they are done, the small town of Stormville, New York will run red. The last ingredient to open the gates of Hell, and plunge this small upstate town into madness, is rain.

And in Stormville, it pours by the gallons.

THE LAZARUS CULTURE
by Pasquale J. Morrone

Secret Service Agent Christopher Kearns had no idea what he was up against. Assigned on a temporary basis to the Center for Disease Control, he only knew that somehow it was connected to the lives of those the agency protected...namely, the President of the United States. If there were possible terrorist activities in the making, he could only guess it was at a red alert basis.

When Kearns meets and befriends Doctor Marlene Peterson of the Breezy Point Medical Center in Maryland, he soon finds that science fiction can indeed become a reality. In a solitary room walked a man with no vital signs: dead. The explanation he received came from Doctor Lee Fret, a man assigned to the case from the CDC. Something was attached to the brain stem. Something alive that was quickly spreading rapidly through Maryland and other states.

Kearns and his ragtag army of agents and medical personnel soon find themselves in a world of meaningless slaughter and mayhem. The armies of the walking dead were far more than mere zombies. Some began to change into whatever it was they ate. The government had found a way to reanimate the dead by implanting a parasite found on the tongue of the Red Snapper to the human brain. It looked good on paper, but it was a project straight from Hell. The dead now walked, but it wasn't a mystery. It was The Lazarus Culture.

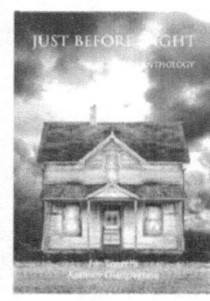

UNDEAD PRESS

UNDEAD
PRESS

Where the Dead
Never Sleep

UNDEADPRESS.COM

CLAN OF THE BIGFOOT

ANTHONY GIANGREGORIO

THE BOOK
OF
CANNIBALS

KISS
THE
COOK

Longoria Grill

EDITED BY
ANTHONY
GIANGREGORIO